A
GATHERING
OF EAGLES

A
GATHERING
OF EAGLES

WALTON YOUNG

WIPF & STOCK · Eugene, Oregon

Resource Publications
A division of Wipf and Stock Publishers
199 W 8th Ave, Suite 3
Eugene, OR 97401

A Gathering of Eagles
A Novel
By Young, Walton
Copyright©2011 by Young, Walton
ISBN 13: 978-1-62564-080-2
Publication date 4/30/2013
Previously published by Goldminds Publications, 2011

PUBLISHER'S NOTE

To my wife, Suzanne

CHAPTER ONE

The last time Prescott Freeman walked through Five Points he had not killed a man. That was two years ago. It was a late morning in June and the white heat of summer was already settling on the north Georgia foothills and Prescott had to squint in the glare of the sun rising from the pavement. He wandered the sidewalks that morning waiting for the train that would take him to basic training at a makeshift army camp south of Macon. He fidgeted in front of store windows and checked the pocket watch his father had given him and thought of the adventure and the excitement a twenty-two-year-old second lieutenant could have.

Now two years later, a brown duffle bag slung across his left shoulder, he limped out of the George Muse Clothing Company and stood at the corner of Marietta and Peachtree streets in the cold rain of Christmas Eve. It was mid-afternoon and the clouds hung low and gray and the rain was like the rain in the Argonne—steady, intense, always there. He smelled the grayness he had smelled before. The afternoon was dark and already the electric street lamps shone a milky white. He watched the sparks that flew from the web of electric wires that crisscrossed Peachtree, Marietta, and Decatur streets and the trolleys that click-clacked along their routes with the faces of shoppers barely visible in the frosted windows.

Prescott was a tall man, with dark eyes and hair—just like his grandfather Jeffrey Freeman; that is what his grandmother Deborah had always said. He never knew his grandfather but he wished he had. All his life he had heard about him so it was almost as if he did know him. He knew about his grandfather sneaking under cover of darkness past the Yankee lines with the woman he would later marry. He knew about his grandfather's exploits on the battlefield, especially at Chickamauga and at Kennesaw Mountain. Prescott's father Thaddeus never wanted to talk about those days; he was always too busy poring over his accounts receivables book and plotting economic strategy.

"The war taught some men how to tell stories," Thaddeus once said to him in the lint-filled air of his office in the cotton warehouse in Rome. "It taught some of us how to make money."

Military strategy of a war fought and lost held no interest for Thaddeus. But Prescott never tired of hearing. Jeffrey was not there to recount the stories but others were and Prescott listened and hoped his day of adventure would come.

The narrow sidewalks were crowded with people with blurred faces rushing past him in the rain. Their arms held packages and he knew they did not see him. His dark, sunken eyes stared upward at the red and green Christmas decorations hanging soggy and limp from the lamp posts. He had lost weight. After the wound it had been hard to eat and he knew the family would notice how the uniform no longer fit. Deep throaty blasts of train whistles escaped from the diaphragms of black steam locomotives at Union Station two blocks away and he thought of the rain and the trains and the cattle cars swaying on narrow tracks all the way to the front. Those whistles were different. They were short, shrill blasts like the scream of a threatened bobcat. He walked north along Marietta Street to Forsyth, where Union Station lit up the afternoon darkness like a Greek temple ablaze with the fire of the gods. He walked into the cavernous lobby. Hundreds of men and women and children hurried to and from the loading platforms. The leather soles of his boots echoed on the black-and-white tile floor and he stared at the white marble pillars that reached upward forever and at the vault of the ceiling with the skylights that were beyond forever. He walked up to the ticket window.

"Where to?" the clerk, an elderly woman, asked.

"Kingston."

Everyone was in a rush. Travelers bumped into him and said nothing and he smelled the dank smell of cigar smoke. Conductors called out hoarsely from the doors lining the far wall, "New York," "Cincinnati," "Savannah," "Chatta-nooga."

"Sir, let me help you with that bag," a gray-haired black porter said. "Where you bound for, sir?"

"Kingston."

"Kingston. My, I haven't been there in a long time."

"I'm sure it hasn't changed."

The porter led him across the wide wooden platform to one of the passenger cars and found him a seat next to a window.

"Thank you, sir," the porter said with a quarter in his hand.

Prescott pulled off his water-blackened trench coat and lay it on top of the duffle bag between his feet. The car was filling up fast with shoppers eager to get to their homes in Marietta, Acworth, and Cartersville. He looked at his reflection in the window and saw the scar on his left cheek. That bullet had not stopped him. The shrapnel that hit his leg did.

What would his father say? Probably "I told you what would happen. I told you you had no business leaving." He wondered what his mother would have said. She had not survived the influenza. He stared at his face in the window and felt the emptiness. He wished he had been there. She had not stood in his way. She had been his ally in the fight before the war.

He leaned his head back on the seat and closed his eyes and thought about the return home. They would want to know why he volunteered to stay in Paris. But they would also want to know about the conference. He would tell them but he could not tell them about Natasha because that telling was more than Paris and he could not talk about it. He knew that his grandfather never talked about his war. He never talked about those things; other people did.

Prescott felt the presence and he opened his eyes. A young boy, maybe six or seven, stood in the aisle next to him.

"My dad's a soldier too," the boy said. "He's not home yet but he will be."

Prescott looked at the boy and at the young woman who stood beside him. He looked at her eyes and knew and in that ineffable moment of not forgetting she knew that he knew and she gave a gentle push to her son and they moved to the back of the car.

"Mind if I sit here?" a short, round-faced man in his sixties said.

The man removed his overcoat. He dropped into the seat. Despite the cold he was sweating and he removed a handkerchief from the coat of his plaid suit and wiped his face with a handkerchief. He held a large brown leather case in his lap.

"Nathan Mulberry's the name."

"Prescott Freeman."

"A captain, I see. You just now returning home?"

"Yes."

"Where's home?"

"Kingston."

"Mine's Chattanooga. Gotta be home for Christmas. I think we'll both make it."

The conductor passed through the car and collected tickets.

"Captain, you need anything, you let me know," the conductor said. "Soldiers are special on this train."

"Thanks."

"You see any action over there?" Mulberry said.

"Enough."

The steam coursed through the veins of the locomotive and the whole car shook. It pulled away from the platform and crawled through the yards and Prescott watched as Union Station faded in the mist. The whistle was blowing long and hard and the steam was building up in the great furnace and at the end of the yards the car shook again. Prescott saw the small frame maintenance buildings at the edge of the yards and soon they were lost in the mist also, replaced by small frame houses. The train headed northwest and the rain became heavier. He saw more houses, bigger houses on narrow lots, their windows ablaze with lights. And soon the houses were gone and there were only trees and the river that awaited them. The car was cold and the passengers chattered as if the effort to talk would keep them warm.

"It's a sorry business, war," Mulberry said and he bit off the end of a cigar. "Never had to fight in a war. Guess I'm lucky."

"Some folks would say so."

"Wilson should have never got us in that mess. That's what I say. That your opinion?"

"He did what he thought he had to do."

"Yeah, well, maybe so. We got enough problems here at home. You know what I mean? We got too many labor agitators. You know? Well, maybe you don't. You've been gone. Well, we don't have to worry about Wilson much longer. Who you supporting?"

"I haven't thought about it."

"Leonard Wood is my man. Great general, good Republican. Of course, maybe you're a Democrat."

The train spewed ash and smoke and rumbled across the Chattahoochee and Prescott saw the muddy water gliding beneath the wooden bridge.

"Marietta! Marietta!" the conductor was passing through the car again. "Ladies and gentlemen, we'll be arriving in Marietta in just a few minutes."

The stop in Marietta was brief, just long enough for almost half the passengers to collect their packages and step onto the platform. And then the train resumed its northwest journey, ready to cross the remaining flatlands and the hills and ridges which waited. Prescott stared at the rain and suddenly saw the twin peaks imperturbable in the afternoon darkness. Kennesaw Mountain thrust its peaks into the clouds.

Jeffrey had been here. The thought made the pain in Prescott's lower right leg more bearable. He knew all about it. His grandfather served for a while under Hardee in the Army of Tennessee and in late June on a reconnaissance he rode practically into McPherson's line along the Burnt Hickory Road. Everybody was so surprised that not a shot was fired. But both sides made up for it. Prescott knew it was raining too—it was a Sunday, June 26, 1864, but then the rain was gone and there was only the insufferable heat. When the battle began on Monday, the worst enemy was not the Confederates or the Yankees but the merciless sun. The dead baked on the field leading up to Kennesaw, and on Thursday both sides declared a ceasefire to bury the dead. Then Johnston withdrew to protect his flank. The dead rested in the coolness of the freshly dug earth. For the living there was no protection from the sun. Prescott had known only the rain, the ever-present rain—and then the snow. The rain washed the blood away. The snow let it sit on the surface and then absorbed it.

"You know, a lot's happened here since we got into that war," Mulberry said. "Business has picked up. I'm in business. Guess what I got in this case?"

"No idea."

"Stock. Not just any stock. No, sirree. I'm talking Coca-Cola stock. Yes, sir. Forty dollars a share and one day you'll be rich."

"Who says?"

"Well, lots of people. Coca-Cola is the rage. Bet you saw people in Paris drinking it."

"Who said I was in Paris?"

"I just figured—"

"No, I can't say I saw anyone drinking it."

"Soldiers are too busy to notice something like that."

"Maybe so."

"Coca-Cola is the future. Trust me on this. I know what I'm talking about. I mean—we just had a big meeting—that's why I was in Atlanta—and everybody was talking about how great this drink is and how people are buying it. Now's the time. Trust me. This is a surer thing than money on Sir Barton. Now's the time to invest in the future."

"I'm always interested in the future. How much did you say it is?"

"Forty dollars a share."

"All right. I'll buy a share."

Mulberry's eyes opened wide. He reached into the case and withdrew several papers with the Coca-Cola logo at the top. He wrote down Prescott's name and address. Prescott handed him two wrinkled bills that he had carried many months.

"This is your stock certificate, Captain Freeman. Now don't lose it."

"I won't. You said this is the future."

"I did and it is. Trust me. Take real good care of it. I'll file the copy with headquarters in Atlanta next week. Sure do appreciate it."

"Merry Christmas."

The train rumbled and rattled through Acworth and Cartersville and the Allatoona hills. The train struggled on the ascent and Prescott knew it would not be much longer. Across the muddy Etowah and across the wide, tumbling Two-Run Creek the locomotive churned. He saw the bend of the creek where he used to fish. When the fish were not biting, he swam. The train smoked past pines and barren oaks and then dormant pastures. The rain grew heavier.

"Approaching Kingston, Captain," the conductor said. "Need any help with that bag?"

"No."

"Nice meeting you, Captain Freeman," Mulberry said. "And thanks again."

The wheels began to squeal and the train slowed. Prescott held onto a seat to keep his balance and he saw the buildings of Main Street flash into view. He stepped onto the wooden platform of the yellow depot and stood at the spot where Andrews and his band of raiders had stood and waited for the tracks to clear. The train pulled away and left Prescott to stare at the town he had left. It looked the same. It was mostly one street, mostly one block of two-story red brick buildings—a general store, a bank, a barber shop, a newspaper, a livery stable, and a hotel. The darkness of early evening mixed with the rain. Light spilled from the windows of the hotel and he crossed the street.

The lobby was small and empty. No one stood behind the desk and the stairs leading to the second floor were silent. He walked into the dining room and set the duffle bag on the floor and sat at a table. He laid his flat garrison cap on the red-and-white-checked oil tablecloth. Connie Lumpkin, a large woman who ran the hotel with her husband until he died shortly before the war, came out of the kitchen and saw Prescott and stopped.

"My God! Pres Freeman! Oh, my God, I can't believe it!" She wrapped her large arms around him and kissed him on the cheek. "When did you get back?"

"Just now."

"And you didn't let anyone know?"

"I wanted to surprise."

"Well, you sure did. Your folks ain't gonna believe it! Guess what? We've got phones here now—at least some of us do. Maggie Sue is the operator. Let's ring her. We'll tell her to put us through to the Hill, provided she ain't asleep."

"No, I want to walk home, Connie."

"Walk? Why, Pres honey, it's miserable out there. You'll catch pneumonia."

"I've seen worse, Connie."

"Well, sure, honey. I guess you have. If you want to walk—well, it's your right. What can I get you?"

"You still serve coffee?"

"For you, darling, I'll brew some fresh. How about some food? I'll cook you up something nice. On the house."

"No, thanks. I'll wait and eat when I get home."

"I'll go make that coffee. It'll take just a few minutes."

"No rush. Take your time."

She disappeared into the kitchen and the words the Hill floated around in his brain. The farm his father owned, the farm that once belonged to Jeffrey, was now called Freeman's Hill; to most folks in Kingston it was simply the Hill. The dining room was warm and Prescott stared into the darkness of the street. The family would probably be sitting down to Christmas Eve supper right about now, Thaddeus at the head of the table. He could see them and they would be wondering.

Connie brought the coffee and set it before Prescott. The steam rose and he stretched forth his hand to feel the warmth. The aroma was strong. Connie waited as he took a sip.

"You make the best coffee in the world."

"What about the French? I hear tell they make pretty good coffee."

"They do, no question. But it doesn't compare to yours."

"God, you know how to sweep a girl off her feet—or at least an old woman. Wish I were forty years younger. Can I get anything else? Piece of apple pie, maybe?"

"No thanks. Just the coffee."

"Well, don't you be leaving any money on the table. The coffee is free. You hear me?"

"I hear you."

He drank the coffee slowly and stared at the street. A Model T rumbled along. It was old Millard Thompson, who lived on the Etowah. Prescott visited his son Chaffey in the hospital which had been set up in a church not far from the Meuse. One wall of the church was missing. A pale yellow light came from the smoking kerosene lamps. Blood-splattered doctors and nurses hurried from one wounded soldier to another. Prescott walked among the wounded, arms in slings, faces in bandages. Chaffey lay on a cot in a corner waiting for the ambulance to take him from the front. A tourniquet above the left elbow had stopped the bleeding; the arm below the elbow was missing.

"Can I get you anything?" Prescott asked. "Water, maybe?"

"No. Just a gun. Let me finish the job the Huns started."

"Don't say that. You're going home."

"What's the point in going back?"

The white-clad American nurses kept walking past Prescott and frowning. They did not want him there; he was in the way. Ambulance drivers, young men trembling with fear, loaded the wounded on stretchers and disappeared. They came for Chaffey.

"There's all the point," Prescott said. "Doris is waiting for you."

"Doris is waiting for a man with two arms to hold her."

"You didn't hear me, Chaff. She's waiting for you."

Prescott stared at the bottom of the white coffee cup. In his mind Chaffey still moaned in the church without one wall. Doris did not wait. She married a drummer from one of the great department stores in Chicago and moved north.

With the duffle bag once again on his left shoulder Prescott walked out of the hotel into the darkness and into the rain. He crossed the railroad tracks and headed west. The rain blew cold in his face and the black countryside opened before him. He could not really see the fields but he knew they were barren and desolate in the winter, yet home to the bobwhite. Beyond the fields he knew where the forests were and where the squirrel and deer and rabbit hid. His boots sloshed in the puddles of the dirt road and he walked between the grooves left by wagon wheels. He tasted the cold rain and wiped it from his eyes.

The wind howled past the oaks and hickories. It was coming from the northwest and he hoped it was blowing the storm to the south. But for now the storm held on and his coat became heavy in the rain. Dogs howled and farmers shouted "Shut up!" and then the dogs became quiet. He walked on the road that was slick like the road leading to the Meuse on 28 September 1918. He and the men of the 1st Division heard the bombardment in amazement. The cannon roared incessantly and they wondered how anyone could survive the screeching shells that hurled themselves into the German fortifications, lighting up the night sky.

"Get that cannon moving!" Prescott said with the rain stinging his face. "The river is just ahead!"

The wheels of the cannon sank in the mud and soldiers pushed and grunted and slipped and pushed some more. Suddenly the air was full of the whistle of rifle and machine gun bullets zipping past them and Prescott and his men dropped in the darkness and crawled toward a cluster of trees to seek shelter from the German enfilade. Bursts of light from the ends of the gun barrels showed the Germans' position and Prescott saw McAdams lying beside the eight-millimeter Hotchkiss.

"Hibbell, fire your weapon! I need cover!"

Both men crouched behind the trees and Prescott waited for a response in the darkness but Hibbell said nothing. Prescott remained behind the tree and bullets splintered the bark, which flew into his face. He smelled the sweet sap. Bullets shattered the tops of trees, which came crashing down on top of the soldiers.

"Hibbell, fire your weapon!"

Prescott shoved the corporal's shoulder and he toppled over. In the darkness with the bullets and bark hurtling past him Prescott saw the large bloody hole in Hibbell's forehead. His mouth and eyes were open in wonder. Prescott was suddenly sick. Bullets ripped into the trees, into uniforms, into flesh. Men shouted and screamed. They called for loved ones—their mothers or their fathers, the girls they loved and promised to marry when they returned.

Prescott ran from the trees to the Hotchkiss, which lay on its side next to McAdams. Bullets skirted the ground at his feet. He rolled McAdams out of the way and a cannon burst tore at the crust of the earth and sent it rising upward. He tasted the dirt and loaded the machine gun and began firing. Overhead he heard the screaming shell from a 240-millimeter trench mortar and the explosion in the German lines. Prescott prayed—*Please do not let those shells fall short*. He did not know how long he fired the Hotchkiss but the barrel became hot and the rain hit it and clouds of steam floated into the darkness. The shells from the 240 continued to fall and the Germans screamed and the earth shook and the trees collapsed. And then he rose and called to his men to charge. His platoon pulled themselves up and ran into the darkness.

He began to walk faster and the puddles splashed against the legs of his trousers. He passed farmhouses with pinpoints of light darting from the windows into the night. He passed the Johnson place, a small frame house where he had played as a child. Shoop Johnson was one of his closest friends. Shoop was the best second baseman he had ever seen. They played for the Kingston team and Shoop hit the home run to defeat Cartersville in '16. Prescott saw the single candle glimmering in one of the front windows. It burned in remembrance of Shoop, who did not make it out of the Argonne.

Prescott followed the road around a bend, past the white clapboard black church and the black cemetery and past Cass Grissom's house. He would have to explain to Cass why Jonas had chosen to stay in Paris. The road began to climb and the duffle bag weighed heavily on his left shoulder. The right leg was burning and he thought about stopping but he kept going, staying between the ruts made by the wagon wheels. The trees were thick along this stretch of the road and he heard an owl deep in the woods. The road became steeper and more slippery. He had to step carefully and then he came to an abrupt stop.

He could see it now—the house sitting on top of the hill, Freeman's Hill. It was a big house, two-story, with one porch sitting on top of the other, but it was not ornate. It had grown up around a central hall. From every window light spread out into the night. He smelled the smoke of the oak and hickory burning in the fireplaces and he knew they would be finished with the Christmas Eve supper and his brothers would be sitting in front of the fireplace in the big dining room and smoking their cigarettes and pipes and perhaps wondering about their long lost oldest brother. Perhaps they would be wondering when he would decide to come home.

Prescott stood in the middle of the muddy road and stared at the big house on the hill and once again wiped the rain from his eyes. Then he heard it—the bark he had not heard in more than two years. It was frantic, joyful. Rap, his black-and-white pointer, came running from the back of the house, barking and leaping against the trench coat.

"Rap, Rap, good boy!" he said and looked up at the porch. He was home.

CHAPTER TWO

"Hey, who's out there causing such a ruckus?" a dark figure standing on the lower porch said. It was Sam, Prescott's youngest brother. "Henry, if that's you again, Mandy ain't giving you your Christmas present till tomorrow."

"Boy, who told you it's all right to say ain't?"

His brother bent to try to get a better look in the darkness. He moved onto the steps, into the rain, staring at the visitor with a bird dog at his feet.

"Pres? God, it can't be! Pres, great God, is that really you?"

Sam jumped the rest of the steps and ran to Prescott.

"Merry Christmas, little brother," Prescott said and he lowered the duffle bag and hugged his brother.

The other brothers, William and Galen, and Prescott's sister, Mandy, were on the porch.

"Sam, what's going on?"

"Who is it, Sam?"

"What's all the commotion?"

"What're you doing out there?"

"Didn't you hear me, Sam? Who is it?"

"Is it Henry again?"

"You ain't gonna believe who Saint Nick has brought home for Christmas!" Sam said and he lifted Prescott's duffle bag.

"Pres? Pres? Pres!" Mandy screamed.

They were all in the rain and Rap tried to stay in the middle of them.

"You folks get out of the rain," another voice from the door said. "We don't make our visitors stand outside."

Prescott climbed the steps and walked across the porch. Thaddeus hovered in the doorway and wrapped his long arms around his son. The grandmother, Deborah, stayed in the hall and Prescott went to her. She was small, thin, with white hair tied neatly in a bun behind her head.

"Hello, Grandma."

"I told everyone you'd be home. No one believed me—especially that ornery father of yours. But I knew. Have you eaten?"

"No, ma'am."

"Well, go upstairs and get out of those wet clothes and I'll have something waiting for you when you get back down."

"Grandma still gives the orders around here," William said.

"You boys, hush. Pres, run along now."

Prescott stood in the middle of the bedroom he shared with William before the war and looked at every piece of furniture. Everything was just as he remembered. Lying in the darkness in the French countryside, listening to the cannon and the whispers of men, he had remembered.

"All your stuff is in the wardrobe just like you left it," William said. "Pres, I swear to God—I can't believe you're home."

"I can't either, little brother."

Prescott sat on the smooth pine bench at the long table in the dining room and Grandma Prescott kept bringing fried chicken, gravy, and potatoes from the kitchen. The family gathered around him and asked questions all at once and he merely nodded his head and ate.

"You've lost weight," Grandma said. "The army obviously doesn't feed you as well as we do. I'll make sure you get some meat on those bones."

"Did you see President Wilson?" Mandy asked.

"Yes, a few times."

"Did you talk to him?"

"Some."

"What was the fighting like?"

Prescott looked at William and chewed more slowly. He then looked at Galen, the next oldest brother, sitting at the end of the table listening but not speaking.

"It was war, William," Prescott said.

"Who wants to hear about war?" Mandy asked. "It's over. I want to hear about the French. What are they like?"

"Let's be more specific," Sam said. "Let's hear about the French girls. What are they like?"

"The French are wonderful people, real friendly," Prescott said. "I think they were a little disappointed we didn't get there a couple of years earlier. But they were grateful we finally did."

"What about this League thing?" his father asked and his gray eyebrows arched as they did when he disapproved of something. "It sounds like a good idea, but I don't think Congress will ever go for it. Lodge isn't going to support anything that Wilson favors."

"You're probably right," Prescott said. "But I agree—it's a good idea. It's something we need."

"I have to tell you, son," Thaddeus said, "that we were all mighty proud you got to be a part of the conference. It was an honor, richly deserved."

"Thank you, Pa."

"Tell us about Paris," Grandma said.

"It's the most beautiful city I've ever seen, even in the rain, and it rained the entire time I was there. During the peace conference I spent all day in meetings and at night some of us would go to the symphony or the opera. I couldn't understand a word of the opera but the costumes were real nice."

"Did you have a girl over there?" Mandy asked.

"Sis, why don't we get nosy?" William said.

"I bet you did."

"I had lots of girls," Prescott answered.

"Tell us about them later," William said. "What I want to know is—are you going with us in the morning?"

Prescott lifted a cup of coffee in salute.

"You better believe I'm going."

IN THE MIDDLE OF THE NIGHT Prescott stood at the bedroom window streaked with raindrops and he reached out and touched the cold pane. The rain was still falling but not as hard. The lonely whistle of the train as it sped through Kingston was the only sound and then there was silence. He thought about his father. He looked a lot older. His tall frame had stooped and the gray hair had thinned and crept away from his forehead. His long fingers trembled.

"Pres, what are you doing up?" William stirred in his bed.

"Couldn't sleep. What's wrong with Galen?"

"What do you mean?"

"He hardly said a word tonight."

"That's Galen. You ought to know. I've seen brick walls say more than he does."

"Go on back to sleep."

The room was cold and Prescott looked toward the pasture. The dim outline of the barn stood in the mist. He tried to describe the whole scene to Natasha and she said she wanted to come.

Prescott walked in the rain along the Rue de Paix and stepped into the café. He closed the glass door and the bell rang. He went to the black stove in the middle of the room and saw them. They sat at the table in small wooden chairs and they looked up and waved him over.

"Pres, you don't look like you're enjoying international politics too much," Dave Cantor said.

Cantor was a large man with a red face and booming voice. He was the Paris reporter for the *New York Times*. Truman, wearing his rimless spectacles, was at the table, along with Seth Morris, an infantry officer from Ohio, and a young woman he had not seen before.

"Pres, you look beat," Truman said.

"Pres, what you need is a drink and intelligent conversation," Cantor said. "We can supply only the drink. Pierre, bring the newly promoted captain a glass of Chianti. I don't think you know our guest. This is—I've forgotten your name. Seth, you brought her. You introduce her."

"Pres, this is Natasha Kamarov. I met her and her family about a week ago at a party Patton was having. Your name came up and, for some reason, she said she wanted to meet you."

"Good evening, Captain."

"Miss Kamarov."

Her English was precise. Her brown eyes glowed with a warmth he had not seen in any woman. Her voice was low. It seemed aristocratic, but he had never known an aristocrat. But her voice, the poise with which she sat and commanded attention from the men at the table, suggested aristocracy.

"She's Russian," Truman said.

"Harry, we would've never figured that one out," Cantor said.

Pierre, the small, elderly owner of the café, brought a glass of Chianti and Prescott lifted it to his lips. The warmth trickled down and he slowly relaxed.

"Well, Captain Freeman of the esteemed 1st, how are the negotiations going?" Cantor asked.

"Dave, I don't want my comments showing up in the *Times*."

"You should feel honored to have your comments printed in such a learned purveyor of information."

"I feel honored just to be in the presence of a learned journalist."

"Nobody's ever called me learned before."

"There's a reason," Truman said. "Gentlemen, lady, I must be going. I have to write a letter."

"Another letter?" Morris asked. "Has it ever occurred to you that gal may get tired of all those letters?"

"No, it hasn't. Good night."

Prescott smiled. Truman walked out the door and the bell rang again.

"Harry's a first-rate fellow," Prescott said.

"He is a romantic," Natasha said. "He is very much in love with this woman. He talks about her so much."

"Bess must be quite a woman."

Prescott wondered why she was in Paris and why she was sitting with these Americans in Pierre's café drinking wine and listening to inane conversation.

"Where in Russia are you from, Miss Kamarov?" Prescott asked.

"Please—call me Natasha. I am from Moscow."

"You speak English very well."

"I speak several languages. And you?"

"I'm American. That means I speak only one."

"The only one that counts, right?" Cantor said.

"I have managed to pick up a little French."

She was in her early twenties and her dark brown hair was combed straight back and fell close to her shoulders.

"How long have you been in Paris?" he asked.

"My family and I emigrated in December a year ago."

"Look, Prescott, I need something for a story," Cantor said. "It doesn't have to be much, but just something. Is this League thing going to make it?"

"It's being discussed."

"Is that all?"

"Talk is all we do."

Prescott walked with Natasha along the Champs-Élysées in the light rain to the apartment where she and her family lived. In the February evening the rain was cold but he did not mind. They talked little. They stared at the street lamps burning furiously into the darkness and again he stared into her eyes.

"I don't understand why you wanted to meet me," he said.

"You are a military hero. Your friends talk about you in such glowing terms. They admire you so much—what you did, risking your life. I wanted to meet someone like that, someone willing to risk everything, someone who had killed Germans."

They stopped at the door to her four-story building.

"*Scheherazade* is being performed tomorrow night," he said.

"I would love for you to take me, Captain."

She opened the heavy door and was gone but the scent of her perfume was still there. It was the fragrance of an exotic land, one he had read about and wanted to visit. He looked at the reflection of his face in the window of the door. He looked at the man who had killed Germans.

FOR YEARS IT WAS PRESCOTT'S responsibility on Christmas Eve to trek deep into the woods for the Christmas tree. In his absence William performed the task. Prescott walked sleepily into the parlor the next morning. A thick cedar tree stood in the corner away from the fireplace, its candles glowing brightly. Thaddeus never liked lit candles on the tree—"too much danger of fire"—but once again Grandma had prevailed. Prescott carried the duffle bag in one hand and walked to the tree and smelled the fresh cedar.

"What's in the bag?" Sam asked. "Are you Santa Claus?"

Prescott sat and opened the bag and withdrew wrapped presents.

"Son, when on earth did you have time to shop?" Thaddeus asked.

Prescott handed out the packages and immediately the brightly colored paper and ribbons were torn. There were silk and perfume for Grandma and Mandy and ties and shirts for the brothers and a wool fedora from George Muse for Thaddeus, who placed it carefully on his head.

"Very distinguished," Grandma said.

Thaddeus lifted a large, long package from under the tree and handed it to Prescott.

"But you didn't know I'd be home," he said.

"Yes, we did," Grandma said.

The package was heavy and Prescott raised it to his ear. He heard nothing. He shook it gently. Nothing moved.

He tore, at first carefully and then not so carefully. Suddenly in his hands he held a Remington double-barrel twelve-gauge shotgun.

"This was Grandpa's."

"He gave it to me," Thaddeus said, "and now I'm giving it to you. I talked it over with your brothers several months ago. I said I wanted to give it to you. They agreed you should have it. Merry Christmas, Pres."

"I think I'm going to cry," William said.

"Me too," Sam said.

"You boys never appreciate a special moment," Grandma said.

"Enough of this talking. Let's see if that old gun still works," Sam answered. "It's time to go hunting!"

"We're expecting bobwhite for dinner," Grandma said.

When Prescott and his brothers stepped onto the back porch, the dogs barked excitedly. Rap ran up to Prescott.

"That dog hasn't been good for anything since you left," William said. "Ain't that right, Galen?"

"Reckon so."

The wind pushed the rain to the south and the sun shone brightly on the frozen specks of moisture that clung to the blades of brown grass. Prescott laid the shotgun with the thirty-inch barrels gently in the crook of his left arm and headed toward the pasture.

"Is your leg all right?" William asked.

"It's fine."

They walked past the barn and crossed the field that led to the Etowah.

"I wish Pa would come on these hunts," Sam said.

"Pa ain't much into hunting no more," William said. "Pres, I sure am glad you're back. Pa's counting on you to help run the business."

"I'm not a businessman."

They spread out across the field where cotton grew in the summer. Only scraggly clumps of bushes remained. Sam was responsible for the left flank, Galen for the right, Prescott and William for the middle. The wind swept from the pines across the field and stung their faces but in this moment of doing what they did every Christmas morning the wind felt good. Galen had just turned twenty, William was eighteen, and Sam was sixteen. Mandy was nineteen and Prescott had a feeling she would be leaving home before the brothers did. The dogs scurried across the field, their noses close to the ground. Rap was the first to pick up a scent. He froze, his back and long thin tail straight.

"This covey's yours, Pres," William said.

"Easy, boy," Prescott said. "Hold the point, Rap."

Prescott transferred the shotgun to both hands and stepped forward slowly and suddenly there was the maddening rush of wings as two bobwhite quail fled their sanctuary and flew skyward. He quickly aimed and the shotgun exploded twice. The two birds floated to the ground. Rap quickly retrieved the first one and then returned for the other. He picked them up gingerly in his mouth and brought each one to Prescott, who reached down and accepted them and placed them in the back pouch of his hunting vest.

"Good boy. Rap, you're the best."

"Well, Pres, you're still a good shot," William said.

"Bet those Huns will agree," Sam said.

"Let's not talk about them," Prescott said. "Galen, you thought any more about college?"

"Sure haven't."

"How about the rest of you boys?"

"Thinking about it," William said. "That's all."

"Me too," Sam said. "Grandma says I'd make a good lawyer, just like you."

"That's because you run your mouth all the time," William said.

"I can't help it if I've got something to say. Ain't that right, Pres?"

"That's right, little brother."

The field swung toward the banks of the Etowah and Prescott stopped and looked at the swift muddy waters rushing toward the Allatoona foothills. Sherman thought he had Johnston pinned along these banks. He was wrong.

"Guess the catfish are safe today," Sam said.

"The day is still young," Prescott said.

They flushed more coveys and the shotguns roared and the game pouches grew full. They heard shotguns echoing in other fields across the river. The wind brought more clouds from the northwest and Prescott studied them and thought about snow. The earth was frozen and crunched beneath his boots. They walked from the Etowah and headed toward Two-Run Creek, which flowed into the river. The clouds thickened and grew grayer and the shadows of the hunters no longer spread before them.

A hill with a cluster of pines and brush rose at the edge of the field and at first the brothers did not see the men but Prescott did. In the Argonne he developed that sense of knowing when others were there that did not belong there. He stared at the figures at the top of the hill—there were three of them and they carried shotguns.

"Who's that?" Sam asked.

William and Galen remained quiet. Prescott stared.

"It looks like the Ledbetters," Prescott said. "Anybody know why they would be hunting here?"

There was no answer.

The three dark figures walked slowly down the hill and Prescott and his brothers stopped. The two groups of men stood some twenty yards apart. Morgan Ledbetter, with his grizzled gray beard and bushy eyebrows, looked much older than sixty. His two sons were with him. Ledbetter spat tobacco juice on the frozen earth and the juice lay there and froze also.

"Morning, gents," Ledbetter said. "Merry Christmas. Good day for hunting."

"Good morning, Mr. Ledbetter," Prescott said.

"Didn't know you was back from Gay Paree, Pres."

"I got in last night."

"Bet you had a good old time over there."

"It was all right."

"This was always a good field for hunting bobwhite," Ledbetter said. "Good place to scare up a rabbit or two. But best for birds. No question. I've been hearing your guns. Sounds like you've had pretty good luck. Don't surprise me none. No, sir. It's a great field for hunting. My pappy loved to hunt this field and I did too. But then I got waist-deep in debt to your old man and he foreclosed, and, being the gentleman he is, he bought it for himself."

"That's all in the past, Mr. Ledbetter," Prescott said.

"Is it, boy? The past rattles in my bones when I get up in the morning. But I guess you're right. The world's changed a lot, Pres."

"Say what's on your mind, Morgan," William said.

"Pres, you've got a young pup there who ain't got good manners."

"What can we do for you, Mr. Ledbetter?" Pres asked.

Morgan Ledbetter pulled his black slouch hat low over his eyes and pondered the question and spat tobacco juice. His sons did not move.

"Like I said, Pres, the world has changed. Bet you don't know the half of it. Well, Galen, I think you know why we're here. I want to know what you're going to do."

Prescott looked quickly at Galen. His brother's face was the color of wet cotton.

"Somebody want to tell me what's going on?" Prescott asked.

The tobacco juice flew again.

"Galen ain't for talking," Ledbetter said. "Just as well. The time for talking is about over. Galen, you hear me, boy? A day of reckoning is at hand and you got to stand up and be counted or face the consequences. You go home now and tell your old man what I said. I want an answer and I want it soon. Galen, you hear me, boy?"

"I hear you."

"Well, you make sure you pay attention. Tell your pa I'm waiting for an answer. Guess we need to get on back home. Been a delight to see you, Pres. Give my regards to your grandma."

Morgan Ledbetter and his sons backed away and turned and walked up the hill and disappeared. Prescott turned again. Galen's lips were trembling.

"I think we'd better head home too," Prescott said.

CHAPTER THREE

Morgan Ledbetter cradled the shotgun in the bend of his left arm and walked slowly along the narrow dirt road. His sons followed silently. He lifted his eyes under the brim of his soiled slouch hat. The sun was just above the crest of the hills. The wind rushed from the pines and hickories at the side of the road. The sons stopped and stared at each other and wondered what to do.

"Pop, you all right?" Josiah, the elder, asked.

"Yeah, I'm all right. You boys go on home. I want to walk to the top of that there hill."

"Why, Pop?"

"None of your business. Get on home now. Your ma will be worried."

The boys looked at each other again but said nothing and walked around Morgan, as if he were a large dark boulder suddenly sprung up in the middle of the dirt road. He crossed a grassy field and climbed the hill. It was not a steep climb but by the time he reached the top he was breathing heavily. The top was clear. The timber had been cut many years ago. Thaddeus Freeman had cut it. He had a right. It was his land.

"No, he didn't have a right," Morgan Ledbetter said.

He stood at the top of the hill and stared. A thin wisp of smoke rose beyond the trees where his small cabin sat in a clearing. He saw in the distance the Etowah. It ran muddy after the rains. The sun was burning a golden path in the west and the wind died and he continued to breathe heavily. He cut a plug of dark tobacco and soon he was spitting juice on the red earth.

"Rotten Freemans," he said and he spat again. "All this land, every bit of it, from here to the Etowah. That was mine. That quail field—that was mine. Thaddeus Freeman had no right to take it. He took advantage. That's what the varmint did. He took advantage. But he's going to pay. He won't get away with it forever. He is going to pay. Just because he's Jeffrey Freeman's son don't mean a thing to me. He's going to pay."

A dog howled and then there was the lonesome call of the bobwhite. The two-note whistle echoed in his brain and he turned and started back down the hill.

"What would Pappy say if he knew I lost the farm?" he asked and waited for the wind to reply. "I wonder if he would've done anything different. No. He was no smarter'n me. Thaddeus Freeman got the upper hand. Pappy couldn't've done nothing different."

He smelled the oak and hickory smoke rising from the chimney and he saw Josiah and Stephen. They were standing in the front yard.

"What are you staring at?" Ledbetter asked.

"Nothing, Pop," Stephen answered and he looked away.

"Nothing, Pop," Josiah repeated.

"Yeah, you were," Ledbetter said. "Make sure you milk them cows. You hear me?"

"We hear you," Josiah said.

Ledbetter climbed the three wooden steps slowly and crossed the small front porch, opened the door, and disappeared inside the cabin. Josiah shook his head.

"I'm worried about him," Josiah said. "This business with Emma ain't good. I don't like what it's doing to him."

"I don't like what it's doing to Emma. She's big, all swelled up. Everybody's talking, whispering. When I was in Calhoun's the other day, I was looking at hammers—you remember, I busted the handle on mine—and I saw some of the fellas near the register. They were looking at me and grinning. Not saying anything, and it's a good thing. My hammer wouldn't have been the only thing busted. You know how people in this town like to talk."

"Don't say that around Pop. He'll beat you."

"You think Galen's going to marry her?"

"No."

"How come you so sure?"

"It ain't all that difficult to figure out," Josiah said. "He's a Freeman. We're Ledbetters. His old man will never stand for him marrying Emma."

"Pop may kill Galen."

"That's Galen's problem."

They headed toward the barn and Ledbetter watched them from the window.

"Those boys are lazy," he said to Myrtle.

His wife stood at the wood-burning stove and fried eggs. Ledbetter liked eggs and bacon for supper and she wanted to please him on Christmas. She was small and bent. She hardly seemed strong enough to lift the iron skillet that sizzled on the wood-burning stove.

"They're not lazy," she said. "They're just young."

"Where's Emma?"

"She's lying down. She ain't feeling well."

"That baby's not coming?"

"She just ain't feeling well."

"She's not thinking that Freeman boy is going to marry her, is she?"

"She loves him, Morgan."

"She don't know what love is. But she's going to know what childbirth is soon enough, I reckon. And young Mister Galen is going to know what retribution is."

Myrtle looked up from the skillet and scowled at her husband.

"Don't you hurt that boy," she said. "If you hurt him, Thaddeus Freeman will make sure you're punished."

"I ain't afraid of Thaddeus Freeman. I ain't afraid of that son Prescott neither."

"You may not be afraid but you'd better respect him. He killed a lot of Germans. He knows what killing is all about."

Ledbetter grunted and dropped into the wooden rocking chair near the fireplace. The embers burned hot and crackled and the heat felt good. He stared at the fire and then at the rest of the room. Only a table and a few chairs. But Myrtle kept everything clean. She set the plate of bacon and eggs on the table. She poured a cup of coffee and set it next to the plate.

"It's ready, Morgan."

"I ain't much hungry."

"You ain't sick?"

"No, I ain't sick. It's just that it's Christmas and I'm tired of being a sharecropper, Myrtle. Thaddeus Freeman has what's mine."

"It's over and done with. You provide. That's enough."

"The roof leaks."

"So did the other one."

"It did? Yeah, I guess you're right. Never could fix a roof leak. Still—it was mine. The roof was mine, leak or no leak."

"Morgan, eat your supper. You like bacon and eggs for supper, so that's what I fixed."

He pulled off the slouch hat and dropped it on the floor. He saw her—Emma, small like her mother, pale, but swollen—outside the curtain that was a door to her bedroom. Her long red hair fell below her shoulders. She shivered in her white gown.

"Emma, you need to put on more clothes," he said. "It's cold in this room."

"Where've you been, Pa?"

She spoke weakly and Morgan stood and walked to her.

"That ain't none of your concern."

"It is my concern if it has to do with Galen."

"You're going to have to forget about Galen," Morgan said.

"Never."

"Emma, do as your pa said," Myrtle said. "Put on some more clothes. You'll catch your death."

"What if I do?"

"Emma, don't talk like that," the mother said.

"Did you see Galen?"

"Yeah, I saw him," Morgan answered. "It was a great afternoon for a hunt. Everybody and his neighbor was out hunting, and I just happened to run into old Galen. We had ourselves a nice little chitchat."

"What did you say to him?"

"Just manly talk, that's all, sweet pie. Are you hungry?"

"No."

"Must be an epidemic then of not being hungry. Well, let me tell you something, Emma. You're going to have to forget about that Freeman boy."

"He loves me and I love him."

"He does, does he? Well, it's Christmas Day and where is he? Has he come here to see you? If he loved you, why wouldn't he come here to see you? Answer me that, Emma."

She lowered her eyes and stared at the floor. She whimpered and he looked away. Myrtle scurried to her daughter and wrapped her thin arms around her. After they disappeared behind the curtain, Morgan walked back to the window. His sons stood outside the weathered barn. They were talking, not laughing, just talking.

"Thaddeus Freeman is going to pay," Morgan said. "He's going to pay."

A log shifted on the andirons and a stream of red sparks flew up the chimney. The sons started for the cabin. Josiah carried a pail of milk in each hand.

"I got nothing to leave my boys," Morgan said. "Nothing."

CHAPTER FOUR

The Freemans sat down to Christmas dinner at the long pine table in the late afternoon. Warmth shot from the flames in the fireplace. Next to Mandy sat Henry Cantrell. A year younger than Prescott, Henry had already begun to lose his sandy hair. Spectacles perched on the end of his nose. He had wanted to join the other young men from Bartow County and fight in France, but his vision was too poor. He looked at Prescott and envied the experience—the adventure—he had had. He did not think he would ever have an adventure like that. Those opportunities did not come along often, and he missed his. But at least he had Mandy, or he thought he did. She did not care about his eyesight or about his hair. She did not care that he did not serve in France. With her he had confidence. Around the other Freemans he was quiet and shy. He always felt Thaddeus was staring right through him and not approving what he saw.

"Henry, you should have seen Prescott today," Sam said. "He still knows how to shoot."

"Yeah," William said, "those bobwhite didn't stand much of a chance."

Grandma Deborah Freeman had fried the quail and laid them on top of the dressing. The platter sat near the head of the table.

"Let's say grace," Thaddeus said. "Bow your heads. And nobody had better steal a quail while I'm praying. Lord, we thank you for this day, the day of the birth of your son. Lord, we've seen war, and now we see peace, and we're grateful to you for it. Thank you for bringing Prescott safely back home. Now please bless this food for the nourishment of our bodies. Amen."

"Amen," the others said.

"Bet you don't get this kind of cooking in Paris," Mandy said.

"You're right," Prescott said. "It's something I really missed."

"We can't get Pres to say too much about the Paris women," Sam said to Henry. "I think he's hiding something."

"When you grow up," Prescott said, "I'll tell you about the Paris women."

"I like the idea of the League," Henry said. "I'm glad you were there, Pres. I'd like to hear about the conference when you have the time."

Prescott looked at Galen. His brother kept his eyes focused on his plate. Outside the wind was whistling around the corner of the house and the twilight was fading into darkness.

"Henry, guess who we ran into this afternoon," William said.

"We won't talk about that," Thaddeus said.

Henry glanced at Mandy and said nothing. Suddenly Galen rose and walked out of the dining room. His boots echoed down the hall and then the front door banged shut. During the remainder of the dinner the family said little. Mandy reached over and touched Henry's hand.

After the dinner Prescott walked past the barn to the shop. It was a weathered frame building not far from the barn. It dated back to the beginning of the farm. Thin strands of clouds swirled across the darkened sky and the wind bore down on the farm from the northwest. The dogs were busy eating behind the house. He walked quickly but silently. He figured Galen would be in the shop examining the tools. That was his sanctuary in times of trouble. It had always been that way.

"Pretty dark in here," Prescott said at the door.

Galen stood in the darkness, his large hands gripping the cold, smooth anvil that rose from the dirt floor.

"What do you want?"

"I'd like to talk."

"There's nothing to talk about."

Prescott struck a match and lit the lantern that hung near the door. A yellow light spread across the floor, where shadows of tools and plows spread and mingled with the light. Galen did not move. His head hung low and his hands continued to grasp the anvil.

"I'd say there's plenty to talk about," Prescott said. "That wasn't exactly a social visit this afternoon. Do you mind telling me what's going on? I get the feeling I'm the only one who doesn't know."

"It's none of your business."

"Galen, when I left here, you were my brother. I don't think that's changed. What have I done to anger you?"

"You do whatever you please," Galen said and he released the anvil. His eyes stared cold and hard at Prescott. "You decide to run off and have some adventure, so you go and do it. You don't think about the rest of us. You don't think about the farm. All you think about is Prescott Freeman."

"There was a war to be fought—"

"—And you had to be the one to fight it—"

"—And I had to be the one to fight it. I make no apologies. That was my decision."

"As for the rest of us—"

"My God, Galen, you're a grown man. My decision shouldn't affect you. What's really bothering you? What's this business with the Ledbetters?"

Galen looked up at the ceiling and smelled the oil and the leather of the saddles. He was tall, almost as tall as Thaddeus, but leaner. The high forehead shone through the shadows. He turned his eyes from Prescott.

"I've been seeing Emma Ledbetter."

"So? As I remember, she's an attractive girl."

"Pa told me not to. I don't know how he found out, but he did. He had a conniption. He told me never to set foot on the Ledbetter place."

"And being the dutiful son you are, you obeyed."

"I got her pregnant."

Prescott removed tobacco and paper from his coat pocket and rolled a cigarette. He lit it and blew smoke into the shadows.

"You know this for a fact?"

"Yeah, for a fact. And don't ask me if it could be somebody else's baby. I've already been asked that question a time or two. It's mine."

"Well, Galen, what are you going to do? Are you going to make an honest woman out of her?"

"Pa said there was no way one of his sons would marry a Ledbetter. He and Morgan have already had discussions. Pa told him there was no way a Freeman would have anything to do with a Ledbetter. Well, Morgan had to be held back. I thought they were going to come to blows."

"Wait a minute. Pa and old man Ledbetter have had discussions. You make it sound like a business transaction. It's not their decision, Galen. It's yours. What are you going to do?"

"With Pa everything is a business transaction. Now that the war is over, all he wants to talk about is finance, the opportunities to make money. You just wait. You're going to hear all the talk. He expects you to run some of his business—maybe the bank, for all I know."

"Galen, what are you going to do about Emma?"

"Pa told me no—I cannot marry her."

"It's not for him to say."

"He's going to offer Morgan a thousand dollars."

"For what?"

"To shut up, to make no demands. If they take the money, they agree to raise the baby themselves. They won't come after me."

Prescott inhaled the smoke and let it drift through his nostrils. The wind howled and a tree limb brushed against the building.

"That's what Pa wants," Prescott said. "Is that what you want? Is that what Emma wants?"

"I don't reckon it makes much difference what Emma and me want. Pa has decided."

"Galen, look at me. Do you love her? Does she love you? Forget what Pa says. Do the right thing. Marry the girl. Don't make a mistake you'll regret the rest of your life."

Galen clutched the anvil and swayed back and forth. Prescott blew out the lantern and went to the door. Galen was sobbing. Prescott had heard other men cry, men he never thought would cry. He had heard them cry in the Argonne, with the cannon bursting overhead and the machine gun bullets ripping apart the earth at their feet. He had heard them cry when they lay on the earth and their blood flowed freely from their twisted bodies. He had heard them cry and now he heard Galen cry and he felt angry and sick.

DEBORAH FREEMAN LEFT THE DINING ROOM and walked down the hall. A glimmer of light shone beneath the door to Thaddeus's study. She walked softly and remembered. She thought of the day long ago when Jeffrey brought her safely from Atlanta to this house. He told her she would be safe here. And she was. She still wondered how he had led her through the Federal lines. They could easily have been captured. But somehow they had done it. But then Jeffrey left. He had to return to the army. Prescott was so much like him. If there was a war to be fought, he had to be in it.

She knocked on the door and opened it. Thaddeus sat behind his mahogany desk, a ledger spread open before him. The lamp at the edge of the desk created more shadows than light. She sat in the chair opposite the desk.

"We'll be able to sell a lot of lumber to the builders in Atlanta next year," he said, and he stared at the ledger as if it foretold the future. "I've read they're expecting a building boom. More industry, more houses. We've got the timber and we can get a good price on it. Then we can invest in more timber. I'm thinking about buying some of the Jansen property. It's been lying fallow for several years. He wants to sell. It's a good place to plant trees. No good for crops, but good for timber."

"I'm not here to talk about business."

He stared at her and then he closed the ledger. He sat back in the black leather chair and interlocked his long bony fingers on his stomach.

"Ma, what is it you want to talk about?"

"Galen."

"What is there to talk about?"

"He should marry that girl."

"Over my dead body."

"The way you and Morgan Ledbetter are going after each other, it may very well be over your dead body."

"If I'm dead, you can rest assured Morgan Ledbetter will be too."

Thaddeus unlocked his fingers and sat up straight.

"There's no way I'll permit a son of mine to marry a Ledbetter. Do you hear? Ma, they're the scum of the earth. They're nothing."

"They're people, Thaddeus. They're poor people. They don't have as much as we do. But that's not necessarily their fault."

"And whose fault is it? Mine? Morgan made choices, bad choices. Emma made a choice. She let herself get pregnant. It was a bad choice."

"Wait a minute, son. It wasn't all her doing. I realize I'm getting a bit old, but if my mind is still working properly, I seem to recall it takes two to accomplish what has happened here. Galen has a responsibility."

Thaddeus filled the bowl of his pipe and lit it. He slumped in the chair and smelled the aroma. It was good tobacco. He had bought it from a tobacco merchant in Rome. He had gotten it at a good price.

"The only responsibility Galen has right now is to do what I tell him to do."

"He's no longer a boy."

"He's still my son. I know what's best for him."

"That's what you said to Pres. He paid no attention. He left. Things turned out well for him."

"He could've been killed."

"He was willing to take that chance. You have to let these boys take their chances. You have to let Galen marry that girl."

"Ma, I appreciate your opinion. I always have, always will. But my mind is made up. Now I must respectfully ask that you let me run this house as I see fit."

"Do you think Abigail would agree with your decision?"

"Please don't ask me that question. She's gone. I believe she would support me—"

"She supported Pres—"

"But I believe she would support me in this. She's gone. I talk to her. I don't know. I've got to do what I think is best for Galen."

Deborah Freeman rose feebly from the chair. Her blue eyes were tired, faded. She started to leave but stopped and faced her son.

"You're so much like your great-uncle. He was a good man. He provided for his wife. He was a wonderful orator, a skilled lawyer. People admired him but they feared him. Many did not like him. Why? He was a hard man. He was all business."

"I wish I had known him. Without him, our lumber business wouldn't be what it is today. He had a lot of foresight. That's what it takes, you know. You've always got to be looking ahead."

"I told your father I didn't think it was a good idea to name you after him. I guess your father thought it would help to heal old wounds. But I think it was a mistake. You've turned out too much like him."

Thaddeus opened the ledger. The discussion was over. She left the study.

PRESCOTT STOOD IN THE LONG, WIDE HALL that ran from the front to the back of the house. Voices and laughter came from the dining room. The door to his father's study opened and his grandmother appeared. She looked small and old and she walked stiffly into the dining room. She was too old to prepare large meals, but she insisted. And Thaddeus did not want to hire help—not when Grandma Deborah cooked for free. Prescott started to call after her but he remained silent.

Light crept underneath the door to the study. He could talk to his father. He could tell him not to stand in Galen's way but it would do no good. The house was large, yet at this moment Prescott felt closed in. The walls were too close. He walked past the study. His grandmother had left the door partly open and he saw his father, head bent over his desk, ledger open beneath his eyes. Thaddeus did not look up. Balances—credits and debits. Prescott walked to the stairs at the end of the hall.

He considered joining the others in the dining room, where the talk and laughter grew louder. Instead, he climbed the stairs. Midway up he stopped and listened to the voices. They were indistinct. They were the voices of another time, another place.

Outside the symphony hall the rain spilled from the rooftops onto the crowded sidewalks below. Prescott held an umbrella over Natasha and she wrapped her arm about his waist. Men and women—many soldiers and their ladies—poured from the hall onto the sidewalk. He was aware only of Natasha. She was here beside him. He breathed her delicious scent. It was the scent of a faraway land, a land he had only read about and envisioned. It was the scent of wildness. There was something about her that was reckless—it danced and sparkled in the depths of her dark eyes—and that something drew him to her.

"Would you like a taxi?" he asked.

"No. This is perfect."

Yellow halos surrounded the electric street lamps, and the wind followed the streets and blew the rain in their faces. He held her closer. They stopped beneath a street lamp at an intersection. Taxis and other vehicles rushed past and splashed water. They jumped back and laughed. He looked into her dark eyes and knew it—knew it for a fact, without question. He kissed her and he knew. He had just met her. But in the rain, in the wind, with Rimski-Korsakov's symphony still thundering in their ears, he knew. He was in love with her. He did not think it was still possible to love, not after what he had seen, what he had endured. But here on the sidewalks of Paris, with lights glistening in the rain, there was love, as if a war had not been fought only a few miles away.

"A princess should not permit an ordinary captain to kiss her," she said.

He kissed her again, and the people on the sidewalks rushed around them. He ignored them. Her lips were warm, full. They felt his love and encouraged it.

"I will make an exception," she said.

They walked across the street, and a taxi slowed.

"*Monsieur?*"

"*Non, mais merci.*"

"It does nothing but rain in this country," she said. "I prefer the snow. I miss the snow. In Russia it snows a great deal. Does it snow in Georgia?"

"Sometimes. Maybe once or twice a winter. There may be a few inches. There may be more."

"That is hardly a snowfall. When it does snow, do you like it?"

"Yes. It is different, something we don't expect. There are many hills where I live. When it snows, my brothers and sister and I haul the sleds out of the barn and go racing down the slopes. And you should see the bird dogs. They chase us. The dogs have as much fun as we do. But I must tell you—I don't think I'd like to live in the stuff for six months."

"You would get used to it," she said.

They stopped at a café and ordered Chablis. Soldiers and women sat around the small cold iron tables. There was loud chatter. Prescott and Natasha took a table close to the window, and he turned and looked at the soldiers. Only a few months earlier these men had trudged through the deep mud and escaped the whistling bullets and the deadly gas. Now it all seemed so long ago. He turned again to Natasha and leaned over the table and kissed her.

For a long time they said nothing. They sat and listened to the others.

"It's getting late," he said. "I'd better take you home."

"Do you have an early meeting?"

"I always have an early meeting."

"Are you pleased with the way the conference is going?"

"Let's not talk about the conference. It's politics and I'm no good when it comes to politics."

"Harry Truman told me the president values your opinions. He said you have made quite an impact."

"Harry's a good guy. He says nice things about people."

"Do not underestimate yourself," she said. "If you were to suggest to your president more involvement in Russia, he would listen."

Prescott lifted the glass of wine and finished it. The door opened and wind and rain followed a man and woman into the café.

"Natasha, at this point there is really nothing else the president can do. There is nothing I can do."

"The Bolsheviks must be destroyed."

"No one is willing to invade Russia. The world is exhausted. We've just finished one war. No one wants to fight another. Look—I know how you feel. I have no love for Lenin. I don't think anyone here at the conference has."

Natasha looked through the window streaked by rain at the people rushing on the sidewalks. They knew nothing about the revolution that had convulsed her country. She wanted to jump from the table and run screaming into the street to make them stop and listen. She wanted them to know about Lenin and the bloodshed. Most of all, she wanted Prescott to know. But she believed him. In the dim light of the small café she listened to his words and knew the allies would do little, but she would not give up hope. There had to be something she could do. Prescott would help her.

"Yes, it is late," she said.

They walked back out into the rain. Her family's apartment building was two blocks away and as they walked, they held tightly to each other. The strength and excitement and passion of the symphony still vibrated in their minds and hearts. Suddenly they stood at the door of the apartment building. Lights shone dimly in the second floor windows. Her family would still be up. Prescott had met her father, Andreivitch, earlier that evening. He was tall, thin. His shoulders sagged. His gray eyes were faded and showed that he had lost much and that he had no chance of ever recovering what he had lost. When Prescott met him, the old man stumbled around the room as if he were unsure of his surroundings. Prescott felt sorry for him. When he looked into the old man's eyes, he saw something else. They were filled with misgiving. It was clear he did not trust Prescott with his daughter.

"I have heard about you Americans," the old man whispered in broken English while Natasha finished dressing. "I have heard."

"All good, I'm sure."

The old man said nothing.

The mother did not speak English. She did not speak French. When Prescott first went into the apartment, the woman seemed embarrassed. She was large. Her dress hung loosely on her. She was pale like her husband. She would not look at Prescott directly. After her few words in Russian, she quickly fled to the back of the apartment. During that first visit Prescott stood at the fireplace in the parlor. The warmth soaked through the wet uniform. The furniture in the room smelled of age and much use. The upholstery was thin around the edges. The family had left Russia with only their clothes and the money they could carry. At the end of the mantel sat a small photograph enclosed by a gilded frame. It was faded and the glass in the right corner was cracked. It was a photograph of the czar—Prescott recalled seeing pictures of the czar in the newspapers—with a young girl sitting on his left knee. It was Natasha.

"He was such a wonderful man," Andreivitch said and he lit his pipe.

Prescott did not answer. Nicholas was not a wonderful man. But he would not argue with the old man. It would accomplish nothing. He continued to stare at the photograph. The expression on the czar's face was severe. The little girl was smiling.

"I want to return to Russia," she said outside the door and the rain came down harder, splattering on the sidewalk. "My friends and I can join forces with Kolchak. I want to fight."

"No, Natasha, that's impossible."

"It is not impossible."

"You are a princess, not a soldier. I do not know your friends. But I imagine they are not soldiers either."

"Someone has to do something to stop the Reds. I am prepared to fight, to die if I have to."

Prescott breathed deeply. He looked into her dark eyes, darker than the night itself, and saw the defiance and determination. Whatever he said would do no good. But he would have to try.

"Please listen to reason."

"I do not want to listen," she said. "I want to act. I have already discussed this with my friends. We are all in agreement. We must fight. Kolchak is a good leader. I am sure the Reds fear him."

"I know nothing about this Kolchak fellow."

"He is as determined as I am."

"You need more than determination," Prescott said.

"I need your help."

A car sped by and the water rose from beneath the tires and sprayed the sidewalk. This time they did not jump back. They did not move. He continued to stare into her eyes. There were tears and she reached out her hand and touched the sleeve of his coat.

"What do you think I can do?" he asked.

"Will you go with us?"

"Natasha, are you crazy?"

"No, I am not crazy. You can get your commander in Vladivostok—General Graves—to help us. You can persuade President Wilson to order General Graves—"

"I can do no such thing," Prescott said. "The president is committed to noninterference. His position is firm."

"You speak like a diplomat," she said. "That is good. You can convince the president—"

"No, I cannot."

Prescott suddenly remembered stories of another country, his country, that had been invaded. As a boy he stood in Kingston's general store and listened to the gray, bearded old men leaning back in cane-bottom chairs and talking bitterly of those days. They had lost on the battlefield. And then their land had been occupied. It took a long time for the hatred to go away. For some of those old men it never did. They carried it with them to their graves.

Her voice was desperate. Her hand clutched his sleeve and he felt her wildness rushing through his body. He tried to imagine those fingers clutching a rifle and pulling a trigger. She would go without him, he knew. He could not let that happen. She knew nothing of war and he did.

"I will ask permission to escort you and your friends to Vladivostok," he said. "I may not be able to get permission.

I think you are making a terrible mistake, but I understand how you feel. Believe me. Perhaps there is something General Graves can do, but probably there is not. You have to understand. If I cannot get permission, then that is the end of it and we must talk of it no more."

The tears were still on her face, but now there was a smile, and it was the smile of the little girl in the photograph who was sitting on the knee of Czar Nicholas.

CHAPTER FIVE

An hour before daybreak Prescott was out of bed. He stood, fully dressed, at the cold window. Above the eastern hills the sky reddened and the thick clouds of the night before were gone, replaced by wisps scattered by the northwest wind. William was still asleep. Prescott lit a cigarette. A dark figure walked toward the barn. It was Thaddeus. Prescott was curious. Usually at this hour Thaddeus was already in his study, poring over ledgers, plotting economic strategy. He was in the barn only a few moments, and then the Pierce-Arrow roared and appeared in the wide doorway and sent the chickens fleeing for safety and headed down the drive to the main road.

Prescott went downstairs and found his grandmother in the kitchen.

"Pres, I didn't expect to see you up so early."

"Couldn't sleep. Where's Pa going?"

"Into town to take care of some business."

She poured two cups of coffee and she and Prescott sat at the smooth pine kitchen table. He drank slowly and realized he had forgotten how quiet the big old house could be early in the morning. Grandma Prescott wiped her tired eyes with her hands.

"Do you want something to eat? There's ham and biscuits."

"No, thank you. Grandma, I know about Galen and Emma."

She sipped the steaming coffee.

"I figured you did. Honey, it's hard to keep something like that a secret. I've heard that Emma quit going into town a good time ago, when she started showing. But I'm sure everybody knows by now."

"Is that the business Pa is going to take care of?"

"He didn't say. I'm sure it is."

"Pa's wrong," Prescott said. "He's right about a lot of things. But about this he's wrong."

"I never want to speak ill of your father, Pres. But I agree. And neither you nor I nor anybody else can do anything to change his mind. Maybe your grandfather could change his mind but I'm not sure even he could. All you Freeman men are the same—hardheaded. You get an idea in your head and there's no changing it."

She smiled. The roosters crowed and Prescott set the cup down.

"Well, the others will be up soon," he said. "I have to leave for a while."

"Where are you going?"

"Just down the road. Then I may go into town."

"Don't try to interfere with your father. It will do no good."

"Thanks for the coffee," he said and stood up.

"Prescott, you are going to stay," she said and she reached out and touched his arm. "I mean—you're not going to return to the army, are you? Your father wants you to stay so much. The others are not much good in business. You are. He trusts you. You're solid. Nobody knows what's going to happen to Galen after this business is over. You can be a steadying influence."

"Grandma, you're the rock solid one."

"Pres dear, I'm not going to be around forever. One of these days I'm going to join your grandfather. The others need you here. I need you here. But I guess there's no keeping you down on the farm once you've seen Paris."

"Yeah, I think the song goes something like that."

He walked to the barn. The earth was spongy beneath his boots. The dogs ran to him, as if expecting another hunt. He went to Sadie, a mare he had ridden for many years, and saddled her. He stroked her mane.

"Did you miss me, girl? You won't admit it but I know you did."

He led the mare outside the barn and mounted. He stared at the two-story house. It was nothing fancy but he thought it was beautiful. His grandfather had thought it was beautiful. He knew because his grandmother had told him. After the war his grandfather had almost lost the house and the farm; somehow he had managed to keep them. The sunlight bathed the double front porches and he remembered seeing his mother on those porches, a broom in her hand. There were no servants. The house was her domain and she exerted authority over it.

Prescott rode down the drive, following the tracks left by his father's motorcar, and headed toward town. The morning was still; the wind had died. He rode slowly and looked from side to side at the land where he had grown up, at the fields which would blossom with cotton and stand green with corn in the summer. The brothers would tend to the crops. Thaddeus had little interest. He looked at trees and saw lumber, buildings, houses. Now the fields looked desolate but that was beautiful too. It was as if Prescott could see their future because he had seen their past.

He heard the distant blast of a shotgun. It came from the Etowah. Somebody was probably hunting squirrel. And he thought of Morgan Ledbetter, the shotgun cradled in his big arms. And he thought of his father, the hatred that coated his words. There was another blast. Somebody was having good luck along the banks of the muddy water.

Not far from the northern edge of town the cemetery sprawled across several small hills. He saw the Freeman plot and he dismounted and walked to the grave. He removed his hat and read the words on the dark gray tombstone: Abigail Stevens Freeman, 1874-1918, Servant of God, Devoted Wife and Mother. The six-twenty whistled past Kingston on its way to Atlanta and then there was silence again.

"I'm sorry I couldn't be here, Ma," he said.

Jeffrey Freeman's tombstone leaned toward him. 1835-1897.

He looked up at the hill across a narrow dirt road. Many small white tombstones marked the graves of Confederate and Union soldiers. Most of them had died during Sherman's campaign in northwest Georgia. Many of the markers had no names. He knew because he had walked among the graves and tried to imagine what the men were like who were buried there. They were probably not that different from the men he had fought alongside in the Argonne. They wanted to win. They wanted to survive. The morning sunlight shot past the barren branches of oaks and hickories and rested on the cemetery and he remembered the men he had left behind, men who would never come home.

Here in the cemetery he was surrounded by the past, echoes of battles and wars fought long ago, and he thought of the future, not his future, but a bigger future. He had fought a war and he had been part of a peace process, yet he wondered what he had accomplished. In Paris he was creating a future, but he did not know what he was creating. No one did. Men had died so that he and others could create a future. Again he looked at the hill dotted with Civil War graves. The Confederate flag was limp. He felt a sense of failure. He wondered what Jeffrey would have done. His grandfather's tombstone leaned toward him but he could not hear any words that it spoke. The words he heard were the hollow words of hollow men who spoke of peace.

IAN BANNISTER BROUGHT THE SHERRY and he and Prescott sat silently and examined the walls lined with leather-bound books. Bannister, already gray at thirty-eight, still wearing the suit he wore during the day's meetings, lifted his glass toward the high ceiling adorned with a brightly lit chandelier. Educated at Oxford, he spoke with even precision.

"Here's to the French," Bannister said. "They bloody well know how to provide for us."

They drank and both men lit cigarettes. On the other side of the tall heavy oak doors conversation was barely audible.

"Well, Ian, you might as well tell me what you want," Prescott said.

"Why are you so suspicious? Why do you think I want something? Perhaps I simply want us to be friends."

"I think it's a little unusual that the prime minister's top assistant wants to see me," Prescott said and sipped the sherry.

"Well, old chap, we've heard the most interesting bit of news," Bannister said. "It seems that you want to go to Russia."

Prescott lowered the glass.

"Who told you that?"

"Prescott, you cannot keep something like that a secret, certainly not here in Paris, where all the world's great powers are congregated."

"How do my intentions interest the prime minister?"

"We have heard that you intend to go not just anywhere in Russia, but to Siberia. My first reaction was—why on earth would anyone want to go to Siberia? But then I thought more about it. You see, as it turns out, we're having something of a problem with your commanding general in Vladivostok. The civil war there is getting more heated, and we think more aid should be given to the Whites. If they do not receive more aid, they very well may not survive, and we know the history of the Bolsheviks and it is not good. General Graves is in a position to do more."

"General Graves is in a position to do no more than what his orders allow him to do," Prescott said.

"If you go to Russia—or, should I say, when you go to Russia—please speak to the good general about this. That's all we're asking, that you speak to him."

"No. You should already know the answer. General Graves has his orders."

"Of course, old chap, I bloody well understand but I had to ask."

Prescott stood and they shook hands.

"Prescott, one other thing," Bannister said.

"Yes?"

"Do not let that Russian girl talk you into doing something foolish. I have met her and she is extraordinarily beautiful. I must say you have good taste. But she is not only beautiful but rash and rash is dangerous in the world in which we move."

"Thanks for the advice, Ian."

Prescott opened the door and walked into the glittering lobby where chandeliers and candelabra sparkled. Harry Truman was waiting, his face anxious.

"What did he want?" Truman asked.

"He knows about Siberia."

"But how?"

"My guess is one of Natasha's friends has a loose tongue."

"Pres, you can't go through with this. It has bad news written all over it."

"Somebody needs to do something about Lenin."

"Not you. And not me. We've just fought our war. We should send Patton. He always needs a war to keep his heart pumping. This is something he'd enjoy."

"Thanks, Harry. If I get through this, you've got to come visit me in Georgia. I'll take you on a quail hunt."

"Just make sure you get through this. Right now I'm concerned."

THE WIND STIRRED AND PRESCOTT PULLED his coat about his throat. The flag was no longer limp. It fluttered over the graves of men who had been killed far from home. They died in war, and Prescott thought about peace—peace—there was no peace.

Walton Young

CHAPTER SIX

There was nothing like a Pierce-Arrow. Thaddeus had driven a Model T often enough but the Arrow was special. Just the feel of the polished wood steering wheel in his hands and the feel and smell of the black leather gave him a sense of power. Most of the farmers in Kingston still rode on wagons or in buggies or on horseback. When he drove down the road, they stopped whatever they were doing and stared. He did not look at them, but he knew they watched and he smiled.

"The only thing special about the thing is it's expensive," his mother had said.

But what did she know? She came from the war generation, from the Reconstruction. How could she appreciate the beauty and power of any motorcar, especially one like a Pierce-Arrow? It was certainly the proper form of transportation to take him to do what he had to do. The drive into town was short, too short, so he drove up and down Main Street several times. He needed time to think. He wanted to be sure he said just the right things.

Clement Acheson's office was upstairs in the building next to the bank and Thaddeus climbed the outside steps with great difficulty. Why doesn't he move to a ground-floor office? He can certainly afford it. Acheson opened the door and led him into his office. Acheson was a large man, larger than Taft as Thaddeus was fond of saying, and he punctuated his sentences with attempts to take a deep breath. The fat was killing him, Thaddeus concluded, but he was a good attorney. He trusted him. Acheson sat behind his walnut desk and Thaddeus took one of the two chairs facing the desk.

"Is he going to sit in this other chair?" Thaddeus asked.

"Well, of course. I'm not going to make him stand."

"He's not going to sit that close to me."

Acheson breathed heavily and stood and moved the empty chair close to the bookshelves.

"Now. Is that better?" the attorney asked.

"These books are musty. You ever open a window?"

"Once a decade."

"I believe it."

Acheson leaned back in the swivel chair and studied his client. Thaddeus was nervous. No question about it. He had never seen him this nervous. This was a sorry business. Acheson did not like it.

"What are you so nervous about?" Acheson asked.

"I'm not nervous. I took the Arrow into town. I'm confident."

"An automobile gives you confidence?"

"Not just any automobile. A Pierce-Arrow is not just any automobile, but what do you know?"

"More than you give me credit for."

Acheson opened the folder on his desk and handed some papers to Thaddeus.

"You might want to take a look at these. I've put the stipulations in just as you said."

Thaddeus adjusted the spectacles on his nose and read the papers quickly and tossed them toward the folder. Then he withdrew his pocket watch and checked the time.

"He's late. I should have known."

"Give him time, Thaddeus. He'll be here."

"Did he say anything about bringing his own lawyer?"

"No, he said he doesn't have a lawyer," Acheson said. "He said he doesn't need one."

Thaddeus laughed and reached into his coat pocket and pulled out an envelope. He tossed it to the attorney.

"Put that with the papers. That's why he doesn't need a lawyer. All he needs is the money."

Acheson opened the envelope and looked inside briefly and placed it atop the papers. Thaddeus checked his watch again.

"Thaddeus, you two should learn to get along," Acheson said. "You're both old men."

"I can still whip him."

"I wouldn't be so sure. Morgan is a large man, maybe not as large as me."

"Nobody's as large as you except Taft."

"Thank you, Thaddeus. I can always depend on you for a kind word. Listen—I need to make something clear. I don't care what your differences are. I don't want any trouble in my office. And don't remind me how much you pay me. I won't stand for any foolishness in here. Do you understand, Thaddeus?"

Thaddeus bit his lip and gripped the chair arms tightly.

"You don't have to lecture me like I'm a child. I'm not going to start any trouble. Save your speeches for Ledbetter."

"There won't be any speeches. I'm afraid the time for speeches is past."

Thaddeus listened. The stairs were creaking. No, it was nothing. He rose and walked stiffly to the window and looked at the street below. Hardly anyone was coming into town this early. He saw a rider stop in front of the newspaper office. Prescott.

"What's he doing here?" Thaddeus said.

"What's the matter?" Acheson asked.

Thaddeus did not answer. His son dismounted, hitched the reins, and walked inside the office. He never understood why Prescott was close to Marcus Stokesbury. He himself did not particularly care for him but, then, he did not care for newspapermen. They were always sticking their noses where they did not belong. He was surprised this whole business with Emma Ledbetter had not been on the front page. He could not help but wonder whether Stokesbury knew. But Prescott would not discuss it. To Prescott family came first. Nothing would change that.

"When you went to Ledbetter's place last night," Thaddeus said, "what did he say?"

"Nothing much. I told him what you said to tell him. Be here early this morning. He didn't even ask why. I suppose he knew."

"Of course he knew. He can smell money a mile away."

"Well, anyway, he said he'd be here."

"Did you see Emma?"

"No. Thaddeus, are you absolutely sure—"

"Yes, I'm sure! Don't ask me again."

The downstairs door opened and banged shut. A heavy weight settled on the stairs and it grew louder and pounded in Thaddeus's head. He turned and stared at the door. The creaking of the steps stopped and he looked at the door knob. Nothing happened. Suddenly it turned and the door opened. Ledbetter stood before him.

"Good morning, gents," Ledbetter's bass voice thundered.

Ledbetter walked into the office and slammed the door behind him. Thaddeus stared at him as he would at a panther that had come down from the hills and had destroyed cattle and needed killing. Thaddeus pulled his coat tightly about him and felt the pistol tucked into his belt.

"Good morning, Morgan," Acheson said, and the lawyer remained seated. "Why don't both of you sit down?"

Ledbetter dropped into the chair facing the desk.

"I was sitting in that chair," Thaddeus said.

"I don't see your name on it," Ledbetter said.

Thaddeus felt the pistol in his belt and walked behind Ledbetter and took the chair next to the bookcases. Acheson did not speak immediately. He stared at the two men, first one, then the other. He looked down at the papers on his desk. He lifted the envelope containing the money and set it aside.

"I think we all know why we're here."

"Let's get on with it," Thaddeus said.

"Morgan, I have an envelope here. It contains one thousand dollars—cash. It's yours with certain stipulations, and those are spelled out in these papers."

Acheson lifted a set of papers and handed them to Ledbetter.

"We can read them to you if you can't read," Thaddeus said.

"I can read," Ledbetter said.

Acheson cut his eyes at Thaddeus.

"Morgan, the main stipulation, which you see spelled out in paragraph two, is that no one in your family can make any paternity claims against Galen. To put it bluntly, if you sign these papers agreeing to the terms and if you accept the money, you and your family are assuming full responsibility for the raising of Emma's child. Paragraph four is also pretty important. It says that no one in your family, including Emma's child, may seek a portion of Galen's inheritance or the inheritance of his heirs."

"It wouldn't do him any good to seek it because he sure wouldn't get it," Thaddeus said.

"That's enough, Thaddeus," Acheson said.

Ledbetter raised his bushy eyebrows and turned toward Thaddeus and Thaddeus touched the pistol in his belt. Ledbetter was silent.

"I've tried to make everything in the agreement clear and straightforward," Acheson said. "Feel free to take your time and read it. We're in no hurry."

"Where do I sign?" Ledbetter asked.

"On the last page above your name."

Ledbetter set the papers on the edge of the desk and Acheson handed him a pen. The pen scratched the last page and Ledbetter shoved the papers toward the lawyer.

"Is that all?" Ledbetter asked.

"That's all. Here's your money."

Ledbetter took the pale yellow envelope and held it firmly in his hand. Slowly he stood and faced Thaddeus.

"If you want to count it, it's certainly your prerogative," Acheson said. "We're in no hurry. Take your time."

"There's no need to count it," Ledbetter said. "You men are gentlemen, some of the finest in Kingston, in all of Bartow County. I'm sure if I traveled all the way to Atlanta, I wouldn't find better gentlemen. Thaddeus Freeman, I want you to think about what I'm going to say. Tell your boy to keep his pecker in his pants and this sort of thing won't happen again."

The red fury rose in Thaddeus's face; the veins in his neck throbbed; he felt the pistol in his belt and his hands trembled.

"Have a good day, Morgan," Acheson said.

Ledbetter tipped his slouch hat and walked out of the office, still holding the envelope firmly in his hand, and again slammed the door. He descended the stairs heavily and the footfalls grew more distant. The door on the first level opened and closed loudly. Thaddeus's hands still trembled.

"One of these days I'm going to kill him."

"Don't talk like that, Thaddeus. You're not going to do any such thing. You got what you wanted. You and Galen are free and clear."

Thaddeus gritted his teeth.

"Yeah, free and clear."

Walton Young

CHAPTER SEVEN

Prescott gently pulled the reins and stopped in front of the office of the *Kingston Times*. He tied the reins at the hitching post and looked down the street. His father's Pierce-Arrow was parked in front of Denton's General Store. Above the store was Acheson's office.

"Here's front-page news if I ever saw it," Marcus Stokesbury said from the open door. "Prescott Freeman home from the Great War."

"Hello, Marcus. I'm making the rounds to see a few old friends, to make sure you still remember me."

The two men shook hands and walked into the office. Stokesbury was not as tall as Prescott. His gray hair was long and combed straight back over his ears. Born and raised in Kingston, he had worked with Henry Grady in Rome and when Grady moved to the *Atlanta Constitution*, he followed. But the pull of the hills of Bartow were strong and he and his wife, Martha, returned and he bought the Kingston newspaper. They lived in the farmhouse where he grew up.

Inside the office, tables and desks were cluttered with papers. Alongside one wall, floor-to-ceiling shelves housed stacks of countless yellowed newspapers. A photograph of President Wilson hung on another wall. A coffee pot sat on top of the hot potbelly stove.

"Can I interest you in a cup of coffee?" Stokesbury asked.

"Yes, you can. I've already had coffee this morning, but I need something to warm me up. The wind is kicking up. It cuts right through you."

Stokesbury poured the coffee and the two men sat at one of the wooden tables and drank.

"I got a wire from Chattanooga," Stokesbury said. "It's snowing up there. Biggest snow they've had in years. As much sun as we had this morning, I'm afraid it's not going to last. The wind is blowing that storm this way. But I'm sure you Freemans have plenty of firewood."

"Yeah. We'll be okay."

"When did you get in?"

"Christmas Eve."

"I need to put a story in the paper. You've been big news around here since the Argonne."

Prescott tried to smile, but it was no good. He drank the coffee.

"I shouldn't have been big news. I was just trying to stay alive."

"Thaddeus told me about the peace conference. That made news too. One of our own assisting President Wilson. Awfully impressive."

"How's Martha?"

"Getting along in years like me. Of course I wouldn't say that to her face. She still thinks she's as spry as a young chicken. We've got our aches and pains. I noticed you're walking with a bit of a limp. You get that in the Argonne?"

"You ever miss Atlanta?"

"No, not really. When I was young, Atlanta was young. We were a good fit. Henry Grady was a great editor to work for. But I always wanted my own paper. You know, life's funny sometimes. As some of us get older, we have this hankering to return to our roots. I guess that's what happened to Martha and me. We love it here. We have a nice little garden in back of the house. During the summer we have all the vegetables we can eat. Of course, she keeps me busy canning. We wouldn't want to live anywhere else. But then we haven't been to Paris."

"Well, you should go."

"We're too old."

"You're not too old. But one day you will be."

"The paper has to be published. It isn't going to print itself. I get a little bit of help from Cy Radcliffe's boy, Simon. And Preacher McIntosh's daughter, Avanelle, writes some stories. I must admit she's a good writer. She may actually have a future in this business if she sets her mind to it. If I ever take Martha to Paris, I think I'll put you in charge of the paper."

Prescott set the coffee cup down.

"I have a law degree. I think I'm supposed to do something with it."

"We already have a lawyer in this town. Besides, do you really want to be a lawyer?"

"Pa wants me to be a businessman. I can't say I want to be a businessman."

"Publish the paper for me and I'll consider taking Martha to Paris. Will you think about it?"

The door opened and Caleb McIntosh and his daughter, Avanelle, walked in. He wore a black topcoat and suit. She wore a dark green coat that matched the color of her eyes. Her red hair brought a fire from out of the cold.

"Prescott Freeman!" McIntosh said. "Welcome home!"

Prescott and Stokesbury stood and the men shook hands. McIntosh stepped aside.

"Pres, you remember my daughter, Avanelle?"

The Avanelle he remembered was a young girl. This Avanelle was a woman. Her face was fair and she smiled.

"Avanelle, you've grown up," Prescott said.

"People have a tendency to do that," she said. "Marcus, you haven't interviewed him yet, have you?"

"No. He's all yours."

"I'm afraid I'm not a very good subject for an interview," Prescott said.

"The last time I checked," she said, "you were the only one from Kingston who assisted the president in Paris. And now you're home. That sounds like news to me."

"You see what I mean?" Stokesbury asked.

"Marcus, we're having a special New Year's Eve service," McIntosh said. "Avanelle has written a little announcement about it. If you can plug it in somewhere in your next edition, I'd sure appreciate it. It's been a rough decade. I thought this would be a good way to say good-bye to it and hello to a new one."

"I'll get it in," Stokesbury said.

Prescott stared into Avanelle's eyes. He knew he was staring and he knew he should not. He looked into her eyes and Natasha came to him, whispering, touching his hand.

"Pres, I know your family is excited to have you back home," McIntosh said. "I can't tell you how many times

Thaddeus has told me he can't wait to get you in business with him."

"Are you a businessman, Prescott?" Avanelle asked.

"I can't say I am."

"I'm sure you have plans," she said. "I want to cover those in the interview. When would be a good time for us to talk? Perhaps this afternoon?"

"I don't know."

"I'll be at the church practicing the music. Just come in."

"The church?"

"Why, yes, the church," she said. "I play the piano during the services."

"You haven't forgotten where it is, have you?" McIntosh said.

"No."

"You're not going to be like some of the soldiers who've come home, are you?" McIntosh said. "It's hard to get them to come back to church."

"Where I've been," Prescott said, "there wasn't much place for church. The last church I was in—one of the walls was missing. It was a hospital. The only singing was the singing of the shells as they flew across the sky. Inside what was left of that church there was a congregation, Preacher, you cannot imagine."

"You're right, Pres," McIntosh said. "I cannot imagine what you and the others have been through. I don't pretend to. But I want to try to help—if you want me to."

Prescott looked away. How could he help? He did not know anything about it. The door closed and the preacher and his daughter were gone. Stokesbury laid a hand on Prescott's shoulder.

"We're all your friends," Stokesbury said. "If you never want to talk about the war, you don't have to. But if you feel you need to, we're here."

"Thanks, Marcus. I didn't mean to be rude to McIntosh."

"He was not offended. He's a good man."

"Does he still umpire?"

"Yes. Are you going to play next year?"

"I haven't thought about it. You didn't tell me Avanelle had grown into such a beautiful woman."

"What about that red hair? That comes from the Irish side of her family. She works hard for a story."

"I can tell. I need to be going. It's been good to see you, Marcus."

They shook hands and Prescott stepped onto the sidewalk. The few farmers who milled about Main Street did not notice him and he was glad. He had known most of them all his life but he did not want to talk anymore. A loud, long, deep whistle signaled the approach of the southbound train. The black locomotive squealed to a stop and thick black smoke rose above the depot platform. Only a few passengers stepped off and then the mighty wheels ground their way into motion and pulled the load behind them. The train was heading to Atlanta. He imagined himself on the train. He knew his father would try to keep him from boarding a southbound. It seemed he was always feeling the need to move and there was someone trying to stop him.

PRESCOTT AND GEORGE MARSHALL STOOD outside the president's bedroom door. The suite was quiet and Prescott was uncomfortable.

"Are you sure he feels like seeing me?" Prescott asked.

"No, he really doesn't," Marshall said, "but he insists."

Marshall knocked and opened the door. The bedroom was almost dark. A lamp on the table next to the iron bed glowed dimly. Wilson was propped up in bed. He wore a white nightshirt and appeared weak and haggard. He had papers spread out before him and he motioned Prescott to sit in the wing chair not far from the fireplace, where a fire burned hot and the flames licked the logs and sent sparks flying up the chimney. Marshall quietly withdrew and closed the door behind him. The room had the smell of sickness.

"Don't come any closer than that chair," Wilson said. "This influenza may be contagious. At least that's what the doctors say. I'm not sure they know what they're talking about. Have you ever known a doctor who knows what he's talking about?"

"I'm not sure I have, Mr. President."

"It's this weather, Prescott. It rains all the time over here."

"Yes, sir. It certainly seems that way."

"A lot of folks are saying I should not have come over here. Supposedly it's beneath the office of the president. What do you say to that, Prescott?"

"I think you did the right thing, Mr. President."

Wilson shuffled some of the papers in his lap, stared at one in particular, adjusted the rimless glasses on his nose, and shook his head.

"What are the other countries saying about the League?" Wilson asked.

The voice was weak and hoarse.

"We have a chance, sir. I think they'll go for it."

"If Russia were here, do you think they would go for it?"

"I don't know, sir."

"I'm sure you have an opinion. After all, Russia seems to be much on your mind these days."

"Has George talked to you, sir?"

"Indeed he has. You should bring this—what is her name?—Natasha to dinner here one night. I'd like to meet her."

"She would love to meet you, sir."

"George tells me she's quite a beauty."

"I cannot argue."

"He also tells me she has this obsession about returning to Russia to fight the Reds."

Prescott did not answer. Wilson lit a cigarette and shuffled more papers and again shook his head.

"Returning to Russia is a dangerous proposition. I imagine you know that."

"Yes, sir, I do."

"And you've explained all this to the young lady."

"Yes, sir, I have."

"George tells me her family was aristocratic. If she returns to Russia, she won't be popular among a lot of people. Does she have any kind of military training?"

"She tells me she can shoot a weapon as well I can."

"Somehow I doubt that."

Wilson inhaled deeply and leaned his head back and expelled the smoke in a steady stream. Then he began coughing. Prescott started to rise but Wilson held out his hand.

"I'm all right. The doctors tell me I shouldn't smoke but what do they know?"

The coughing subsided and Prescott wanted to move the chair away from the fire; it was too hot but he remained stationary.

"George tells me you want to escort the young lady and some of her friends back to their homeland," Wilson said.

"Yes, sir. We can meet with General Graves in Vladivostok and from there join a contingent of Whites. At least that's our plan, sir."

"Prescott, it's foolhardy. You're asking to get yourself killed."

"I made it through the Argonne, Mr. President. I can make it to Siberia and back."

"Prescott, the situation in Russia is complicated. I'm sure I'm not telling you anything you don't already know. Not only do we have troops in Vladivostok, but so do the British and the French and the Japanese. I think it's important that Russia's territorial rights be respected. As long as we're there, I don't think anybody will try to annex a part of Russia, if you follow me. General Graves has strict orders to maintain our neutrality. As a result, some of our friends are a little upset. They think he should be helping the Whites. Despite pressure, he has followed my orders to the letter. I don't mind saying, Prescott, that your desire to go there and become involved with the Whites can compromise our neutrality."

The two men studied each other. In the firelight the president's face was flushed and he coughed again. Then he lifted one of the papers and motioned to Prescott to take it.

"It's a letter from me to General Graves," Wilson said. "Prescott, I don't want to release you for this journey—you're much too valuable to me here—but George tells me you believe this is something you must do, so I'm not going to stand in your way. I really don't think there's anything your Russian friend can do to affect the outcome of the civil war. Nevertheless, I'm telling Graves to treat you with all due respect and provide whatever equipment you need for your travels in Siberia. General Graves is a fine officer. More than that, he is a fine man."

"Thank you, sir."

"You also have to understand that if the Reds capture you, they'll consider you a spy and execute you. There won't be anything I can do to stop them. You understand?"

"Yes, sir."

He lifted another piece of paper but it did not seem worth the effort; he let it fall on the bed.

"I've been hearing stories that Senator Lodge is mounting an offensive against the treaty, especially against the League," Wilson said and he removed the glasses and rubbed the already red eyes. "You're a military man. I don't guess you keep up with political shenanigans."

"Soldiers have ears, Mr. President. I've heard the same stories."

"This League means a lot to me, Prescott, a whole lot. We can't have another war like the one we just went through. There's only so much horror that the world can endure. You were there in the thick of it. You know what I'm talking about."

"Yes, sir."

"If only I could make Lodge and his cronies see. Any chance you can take him to Siberia with you?"

Wilson smiled.

"No, I didn't think so."

There was a sharp knock and the door opened. An American nurse in a white uniform marched into the room and spread out her authority like a blanket. It was apparent that she was accustomed to giving orders, and it did not matter that the patient was the president. She scowled at Prescott and went immediately to the bed. She poured a dark liquid into a spoon.

"Mr. President, it's time for your medicine."

She thrust the spoon into his mouth and he withdrew his face in disgust. She poured another spoonful, which he accepted reluctantly.

"Don't you have any medicine that tastes halfway decent?" he asked.

"It's the price you pay for being sick," she said and there was no smile.

She took a white cloth from a pocket in her apron and wiped the corners of his mouth. She frowned again at Prescott and then marched out of the room.

"If that's the price I pay for being sick," Wilson said, "I'd better get well. You know, Prescott, when I practiced law in Georgia, I heard about your grandfather. Let's see. What was his name? Jeffrey, Jeffrey Freeman, I believe."

"Yes, sir."

"Another fine soldier."

"Yes, sir."

"Just a different war."

"Yes, sir."

"Different, yet the same," Wilson said and the drowsiness crept into his sunken eyes.

"I'd better go," Prescott said. "Thank you for the letter, sir."

"Just don't get yourself killed. And hurry back. We may still be here this time next year."

Wilson's chin sank upon his chest and Prescott walked out of the bedroom. In the anteroom George Marshall sat on a small sofa and stood when Prescott appeared.

"Well, Captain Freeman," Marshall said, "did you get what you were hoping for?"

"Indeed I did, Captain Marshall," Prescott said and he held up the letter. "It appears I will be going to Russia."

"Prescott, you're a fool. You know that, don't you?"

"So I've been told."

They went to the elevator and the operator pulled shut the brass-colored screen and door. The elevator jerked into motion and quickly descended. Prescott and Marshall walked into the lobby, where Natasha was sitting by the winding staircase. She jumped to her feet and ran to meet them.

"Did you see the president?" she asked.

"Yes, love, I saw the president," Prescott said.

"He's making Prescott the vice president," Marshall said. "That means he leaves for Washington tomorrow."

Natasha's eyes widened with concern and Prescott laughed.

"Don't believe this fellow," Prescott said.

"I was lying," Marshall said. "He doesn't leave till day after tomorrow."

Marshall returned to the elevator and Prescott took Natasha's arm and they walked into the February cold and rain.

"Is it really true you are going to Russia with me?"

"Yes, dearest, it is true. Everyone tells me I'm crazy."

"Are you crazy?"

"Yes, I'm crazy."

He held her tightly and they walked beneath the electric street lamps that produced pale halos in the rain. They walked slowly and he thought of many things—whether he should write to his family, whether Wilson would recover—he had seen what the influenza could do—and whether the trip would really be that dangerous. It was not as if he would be going into combat. But if there were fighting, then he would fight. He had fought before and he would fight again.

They came to their café—they had come here so many times in the past few weeks that they considered it theirs—and went inside to escape the rain. It was early; the theater patrons had not spilled onto the street. They ordered Chianti and drank in silence.

PRESCOTT STOOD BESIDE HIS HORSE. His father's Pierce-Arrow was still parked up the street. Suddenly Morgan Ledbetter descended the steps from Clement Acheson's office. When he reached the sidewalk, he walked swiftly, surely, as if he had accomplished something. Not long afterward Thaddeus came down the steps. The car thundered and disappeared.

Then it was Acheson's turn to leave the office. Despite the cold he did not wear a coat. He rumbled along the sidewalk toward the hotel. He saw Prescott and stopped.

"Welcome home, Pres," Acheson said.

"Good morning, Clement. I just saw Pa and Morgan Ledbetter come out of your office."

"Yeah. They ran into each other. Strange coincidence, wouldn't you say? I need a piece of apple pie and a cup of coffee. Join me?"

"No thanks."

Acheson went into the hotel dining room and Prescott mounted the horse. The sunshine had vanished. The wind was forcing the clouds, thick and gray, from the northwest. They swirled and grew stronger. The snow was coming. It would have made Natasha happy.

Walton Young

CHAPTER EIGHT

Caleb McIntosh pulled on the reins and the buggy stopped in front of the Ledbetter shack. He helped Avanelle down and they went to the door. Myrtle opened the door and stepped back.

"Preacher, what are you doing here?"

"I thought we should come and see how you're doing. Elizabeth sent some of her pickled peaches."

He held the Mason jar out and Myrtle was at first reluctant, but then she took it. The room was smoky. The fireplace did not draw well.

"Morgan ain't here," Myrtle said.

"How is Emma?" Avanelle asked.

"She's behind that curtain. I reckon you can see for yourself."

Avanelle pulled back the curtain and stepped into the room. Emma lay on the bed beneath a frayed patchwork quilt. A white slop jar was visible beneath the bed. The room had no window and Avanelle felt as if the walls were closing in, but she smiled.

"Why did you come?" Emma asked.

Her voice was weak. Her hands, white and trembling, clutched at the edge of the quilt beneath her chin.

"I wanted to see if there's anything I can do."

"There's not."

"Do you feel the time is getting close?"

Emma nodded and the tears began. Avanelle rushed to the bed and sat. She removed a handkerchief from her coat pocket and wiped the tears.

"Where is Galen? Why won't he come?" Emma asked.

"I don't know," Avanelle said.

She did not know what to say. The town knew what had happened, so there was nothing to hide. She did not understand why Galen refused to come.

"Has your pa sent for the doctor?"

"No."

"Do you want me to?"

"No. Pa will fetch him when he thinks it's time."

"Emma, I'm not sure your pa knows much about these things. Please, let me—"

"No, Avanelle, I appreciate it, but my family will take care of everything."

Caleb McIntosh came into the room and tried to smile. It was difficult.

"Emma, would you like me to say a little prayer?" he asked.

"No. No, please."

"All right. Avanelle, we'd best be going."

She stood and took Emma's left hand between both of hers and squeezed gently. She and her father turned and walked past Myrtle and out the door.

Myrtle stood in the door and stared at the buggy. It grew smaller and disappeared around the bend in the road. She looked up at the sky and did not like what she saw. The clouds were piling up. Snow was coming. If the baby came.... Myrtle closed the door and listened. Emma was calling.

McIntosh and Avanelle headed toward town. The mare was taking her time, but the preacher did not care to hurry her. Avanelle stared into the distance, past the oak- and hickory-lined slopes of the hills. There was grayness in the air. She saw it and smelled it.

"I feel like riding up to the Hill and giving Galen a piece of my mind," she said.

"I would not recommend it. Don't stick your nose where it doesn't belong."

"But somebody needs to do something. Emma is about to have a baby—Galen's baby—and he should be there. Old man Ledbetter should go with his shotgun. You should do the marriage ceremony."

McIntosh laughed.

"Now that would be a story for the *Kingston Times*. Old Marcus should give you a raise for a story like that."

"Papa, I'm mad. You don't think Prescott is like his brother, do you?"

"No. He and Galen are different. Pres is his own man. Why do you ask?"

"I was just curious, that's all."

"Curious as a newspaper reporter or as an interested young lady?"

"Papa, there are some snowflakes."

"I think it's going to be a storm this time. Usually the storms don't come till January or February. This one's a bit early."

"Prescott is troubled."

"I know. A lot of them who have come back are troubled. But Pres—well, even more so, as it appears to me. It's going to take time for him to—to readjust. All the stuff that's going on with his family isn't going to help matters."

She clung to her father's arm, smiled, and looked down the road. If his family could not help, perhaps someone else could.

Prescott mounted his horse, headed down Main Street, and followed the tracks of the Pierce. A bobwhite whistled in a distant field. It was a lonely call borne on the northwest wind. Then he drew the reins tight and the horse stopped. He listened to the other call. It was the shrill call of the screech owl. In the middle of the day it was not a good sign. That was what his grandmother had always told him.

"You hear a screech owl in the middle of the day and somebody is going to die," she had said.

He had heard it before and his grandmother had always been right. He heard it in France but only in his dreams and the killing soon followed. He stared at the barren oaks on both sides of the road and wondered which tree housed the bird. He listened but the wind was playing tricks with the shriek.

Rumbling down the dirt road was a wagon pulled by two mules, and Cass Grissom hollered "Whoa!" and the mules stopped.

"Pres Freeman! Can't believe my eyes!"

"Hello, Cass. Merry Christmas."

Cass turned his black face toward the sky and listened. The screech owl had grown silent.

"I guess you heard that," Cass said.

"Yeah, I sure did."

"Never like to hear that in the middle of the day. Oh well. Not a thing we can do about it, is there?"

"No, I'm afraid not."

"When did you get home?" Cass asked.

"Christmas Eve."

"What a Christmas gift for your family."

"I don't know about that."

Prescott reached into his coat and pulled out a tobacco pouch and paper and offered a cigarette to Cass but the old man declined. Prescott cupped his hands to shield the match from the wind.

"I wish my boy was home for Christmas," Cass said and he removed his dark hat and ran his fingers through the gray hair.

"I was planning to stop by your place."

"You have word from Jonas?"

"I just wanted to tell you about the last time I saw him. It was in February. He was doing fine."

"That's what he wrote," Cass said and he put the hat back on. "He ain't one to write much, but he said he was doing fine. He could be doing fine here, Pres. I just don't understand it. Why won't he come home?"

"He likes it over there, Cass. Paris is a wonderful city."

"I don't want nothin' to do with cities. Oh, they're beautiful, all right. But they're sinful. I'm afraid my boy is going to get caught up in something bad."

Prescott puffed the cigarette and the wind sent the smoke scurrying away. He stared at the deep furrows in Cass's high forehead. Grissom had always looked old, but he was the best farmer in Kingston. He was a farmer everyone, even Thaddeus, came to for advice. Cass knew a lot about rotating crops. He had cautioned Thaddeus about relying too heavily on cotton because the soil just could not take it year after year. But Thaddeus seldom listened to advice, even when he sought it.

"Jonas can take care of himself. You did a good job raising him, Cass. You've got nothing to be ashamed of. Give him some time. Jonas just has to find his way. No one can do it for him."

"I just hope that screech owl ain't calling his name."

Cass urged the mules onward. At first they did not want to move but he cracked the reins across their backs and they started forward. Prescott turned in the saddle and observed the old black man, his body bent against the wind.

A wall of thick gray clouds was building in the west and hanging low over the hills. Prescott neared the cemetery and saw the Pierce-Arrow parked at the side of the road. Thaddeus was standing at the family plot and did not hear his son approaching. Prescott dismounted and cleared his throat. Thaddeus turned around.

"Pa, you all right?"

"Yeah, I'm fine, Pres. Sometimes I just need to stop here and have a little chat with your mother."

"I saw your car in town."

"I had some business to take care of."

"It must have been pretty important."

"It was. But it's all taken care of now. There's nothing else to worry about."

Prescott nodded and returned to his horse. He mounted and Thaddeus stood facing the monument. The wind shook the naked branches of the oaks and hickories and the screech owl shrieked again.

The wind shot across the pastures and open fields and the clouds grew thicker and more numerous. The air was cold and moist and the first flakes of snow, small like pinpoints of white light, began to fall. At first it did not even look like snow but then the flakes became bigger and fluffier. He rode slowly past farmhouses and the bird dogs and hounds stood on the front porches and barked. He liked the snow. It was better than the rain.

LAUGHTER AND CONVERSATION FILLED the small café. Patton raised a glass of champagne and the other officers joined in. The fire in the black stove burned hot but Prescott was still wet and cold. It would never stop raining.

"Here's to Russia," Patton said loudly. "May God protect her now that Prescott Freeman is about to invade!"

"I'll drink to that," Marshall said.

Truman's glass remained on the round table.

"Harry, what's the matter?" Patton asked.

Truman removed his spectacles and wiped them on his handkerchief and then put them back on, as if to get a better look at Prescott.

"Pres, you'd better be careful," Truman said. "That girl will get you killed."

"Don't worry, Harry," Patton said. "He'll be careful. Look what he did to the Germans. God, I wish I could have been there, Pres! I wish I could have seen it."

"Harry, why don't you play us something?" Prescott asked.

Truman looked around and saw the old scarred upright tucked in a far corner of the café. He adjusted the spectacles on his nose again, stood, and walked briskly to the bench and sat. Then his fingers were moving briskly across the keys and the café was alive with a waltz. Patrons at the other tables stopped drinking and talking and listened to the music flow as powerfully as the Danube itself. Truman finished and bowed to the applause.

"You know, Harry, that's what you should do," Marshall said. "When you get back to Missouri, you need to become a musician."

"He's going to do whatever this Bess woman tells him to do," Patton growled and he poured another glass of champagne.

"What are you going to do?" Prescott asked.

"I don't know for sure," Truman said. "I've given some thought to a haberdashery."

"No, that's no good," Patton said. "Selling clothes? That's not for you, Harry. Why don't you stay in the army? You're a good officer. You distinguished yourself on the battlefield. You're a true leader of men. And that's what this army needs. Are we all in agreement? Harry, look at the rest of us. We're all going to stay in the army. Right, gentlemen? George, Prescott?"

"Yeah, I'm staying in," Marshall said.

They stared at Prescott.

"Well, Pres?" Patton asked. "You're not planning to stay in Russia the rest of your life, are you? I mean—when you get back, you're going to stay in the army. Right? I'm sure this Russian lady will have no objections. Of course, after you whip the Reds, she may set you up as the new czar. That's still the military in a way. You'll get to wear a uniform."

"I'm like Harry. I don't know for sure. My pa is expecting me to help with the business."

"Let me tell you something about business. It will be there forever," Patton said. "There are wars to be fought, gentlemen. And we're the ones to fight them."

Prescott lowered his glass and set it gently on the table and heard the screams of his men in the forest and felt the earth explode beneath him. Patton wanted to be there. Yes, he should have been there.

"I think I've fought enough," Prescott said.

"You think there's no fighting in Russia?" Patton said. "You think the Whites and Reds are really good friends just having a little disagreement? No, sir. It's not that way at all. And you're going to be right in the middle of it. Not a good spot for a man who has fought enough. It's civil war, Pres. And we all know something about civil war. It gets a bit nasty at times."

"Although I hate to admit it, Patton is right," Truman said. "It's going to be dangerous. I'm aware of our position of neutrality. But you may have no choice—you may have to fight."

Prescott lifted the glass and downed the drink. The warmth sank smoothly.

"Well, if I have to, then I will."

Prescott left the officers and walked in the rain to Natasha's apartment. Her father sat beside the fire and read a Russian-language newspaper and did not speak; he only nodded his head in greeting. The mother said something in Russian, smiled almost bashfully, and disappeared into the kitchen. Natasha led him to the sofa near the window in the parlor. The fire danced in her eyes and her face was flushed.

"You've been standing too close to the fire," Prescott said.

"No, I'm just excited, darling. I've been making a list of the things I must take."

She held a piece of white paper before him and he took it. She had written it in French, so he was able to read it.

"This is not a vacation," he said. "You won't need this many dresses. We must travel light."

Disappointment clouded her face and she took the list back.

"Pres, you must remember. I am a princess."

"I remember. The Reds do not."

She nodded and tore the paper in half. He had noticed that the list did not include weapons. No matter. He would take care of those.

They left the apartment and wandered the sidewalks. The rain was now only a light mist and her face still glowed red in the pale lamplight. The streets were crowded and taxis frequently stopped and the drivers offered a lift but they wanted to walk. He held her close to him and he felt the breathing of her body through her coat. He was crazy to agree to this. Everyone was telling him so and now he was joining in the chorus. He should not put her life in such danger but he could not refuse her request. His own land had been ripped apart by civil war. Brother had killed brother. Families chose sides and the sorrow still lingered. His grandfather had fought. He opposed slavery. He disdained those who owned slaves. But he had fought. It was his land. Natasha and her friends wanted to do what they could to reclaim their land. He wished her father would speak up and say something to dissuade her. He wished her mother would try. Neither did anything. He decided he did not like them.

Outside the opera house the patrons were emerging. Many officers, whose names he did not know, whose faces he did not recall, and their ladies descended the steps. Suddenly one of the men spoke his name.

"Pres, I can't believe it's you," a young lieutenant said and he came down the steps with a lady holding firmly onto his left arm.

"Jonas, where have you been?" Prescott asked. "I've looked around but nobody knew where you were."

"Out in the countryside. I ain't the war hero you are. They're just now letting me come into the city for some relaxation. I want you to meet Mademoiselle Mathilde Cavalier."

"*Bon jour,*" Prescott said. "This is Natasha Kamarov. Natasha, this is Jonas Grissom. He's from my hometown."

"*Bon jour, monsier. Je ne parle—*"

"Don't worry, honey," Jonas Grissom said. "I'll do the talking for you."

"What is that on your shoulder?" Natasha asked.

"That's a black buffalo," Jonas said and he turned so that the lamplight shone on the patch. "I'm in the 92nd, the meanest division in all of France. You see that red 1 on Pres's shoulder? All that means is he's the first one on the scene after I've cleaned up the mess. He'll tell you he's the best shot in Bartow County. But don't believe it. I am."

"I see you're just as modest as ever."

"Pres, I got great news. I'm mustering out next week."

"Congratulations, Jonas. Your pa will be happy to hear it."

"I ain't going home," Jonas said and he smiled at the woman beside him. "Me and Mathilde—well, we've got things to do."

"I'm sure Cass is expecting—"

"Why should I go back to Georgia?" Jonas Grissom asked and Mathilde Cavalier released her grip. "I mean— what is there for me? No more going to the back door for me. Over here I can march right up to the front door and no one says a word."

"Jonas, when you came to our place, you never had to go to the back door."

"I know. And I'll always appreciate it, Pres. But I don't have to tell you how it is. There's no sugarcoating it. I ain't no slave. And that's how I'm treated back home. Here it's different. Just look at sweet little Mathilde here. Do you think she cares what color I am? No, sir. She can't even say black in English. And that's fine with me. I need to see a little bit of the world. Paris is a great place to start. Wouldn't you agree, Miss Kamarov?"

"Yes, certainly."

"I'll write a letter to Pa. I ain't too good with letters, though. Pres, when you go home, maybe you can explain it to him."

"I'll do what I can," Prescott said.

Jonas Grissom and Mathilde Cavalier walked down the sidewalk and disappeared in the mist. Prescott watched them.

"He seems like such a nice man," Natasha said. "I would like to ask him questions about you when you were young."

"You can ask me."

"But I am sure he will tell the truth."

Jonas and Mathilde were gone. But Prescott still saw a young black man who wanted to play first base. His teammates hesitated.

"Marietta won't play us."

"Either he plays or I don't pitch."

The Marietta team adjusted their short-billed caps and looked at each other and ran their cleats across the dusty field. Jonas stood near home plate. McIntosh removed the wire mask and approached the infield.

"I don't know about a man of God calling balls and strikes," the Marietta second baseman said.

"Who better to call balls and strikes?" McIntosh said. "What I say out here carries divine authority. You got a problem with that, son? This July heat isn't getting any cooler, gentlemen. What are we waiting for?"

The visitors looked toward Jonas and Jonas remained stone-faced, storing up remembrances of the images before him.

"I have to tell you boys that Jonas Grissom is the best left-handed hitter I've ever seen," McIntosh said. "Of course, if you're afraid—"

"We ain't afraid of you," the Marietta center fielder said. "We ain't afraid. Sure, we'll play you. It'll be just that easier to whip you."

After Prescott finished his warm-up pitches and the ball was tossed around the infield, Jonas approached the mound. He and Prescott looked at each other but neither spoke. The hint of a smile curled around Jonas's lips and he returned to first base.

"Play ball!" McIntosh said.

Prescott pitched and Jonas played first and hit a double and a home run. Kingston won.

"Yes, he will tell the truth," Prescott said. "He's a good man. Let's go to the café."

Walton Young

CHAPTER NINE

The snow came down in bigger flakes and the wind blew them into swirls. Streaks of white lined the wagon ruts and the ditch at the side of the road. Along the outstretched barren limbs of oaks the snow clung. The wind stung Prescott's face but he did not mind. There had been too much rain. The snow was welcome. And Natasha had liked the snow. From it she pulled heat and energy and the will to do the impossible.

He decided not to return to Freeman's Hill; instead, he urged the mare toward the Etowah. As a boy he watched the snows of January and February. They came quickly but not unexpectedly. The old folks came out of their houses and barns and stores and thrust their hands into the pockets of faded blue overalls and studied the gray northwest sky and listened to the whine of the wind and they knew. Snow was coming. Prescott thought about those days when the old men and women were so close to the land from which they came that they knew the intentions of nature. Thaddeus did not know. He did not care to know. As a boy Prescott watched the snow. It seldom came but when it did, it was something special to be admired and enjoyed. It slid effortlessly from the grayness of above into the grayness below and disappeared into the fast moving waters of the Etowah.

The road became slippery and twice the mare stumbled but she regained her footing and he rode across the barren field where snow sprinkled the undergrowth. He came upon a grassy rise and looked down at the river. Above the pines and hickories on the far side of the bend dark smoke rose, did battle with the wind and became one with the grayness. He followed the river toward the bend, where the muddy water dropped suddenly against worn, gray granite boulders and fell into a shallow pool. In the pool the trout waited. He knew. He had fished there many times in the hot summer months. Beyond the pool the river regained its energy and plunged south toward the Allatoona foothills.

Smoke rose from the lone chimney of a small cabin hidden in the woods only a hundred yards or so from the river. Verlon Freeman, his uncle, lived here. Prescott tied the reins to a low-hanging, snow-covered branch near the small front porch. Verlon was standing at the open door and smoking a pipe. He was older than Thaddeus, taller and leaner. His high forehead was deeply lined. Exposure to the sun had darkened his face, neck, and hands. Long white hair curled over his ears and fell nearly to his shoulders.

"So you decided to come see your old uncle."

"Hello, Uncle Verlon. You knew I was back home?"

"Even though everyone seems to think I'm something of a hermit, I hear things. Come on in. The snow ain't letting up."

Prescott climbed the two wooden steps and walked into the room. It was not a large room but it was big enough to serve as a sitting room, bedroom, and kitchen. He pulled off his wet coat and sat in a rocking chair close to the fire. There was no couch. A fire crackled in the fireplace and the warmth felt good. Prescott had sat in this cabin many times on cold winter days and listened to the stories his uncle told about farming, but mostly about hunting and fishing. Verlon knew things about the land that Prescott feared was being lost. Thaddeus did not know those things. Prescott's brothers did not know them. Verlon sat on the white iron bed and puffed on the pipe.

"Snow came a little early this year," Verlon said and he crossed his legs. "Caught me by surprise."

"Nothing catches you by surprise."

Verlon smiled and released the pipe smoke into the air. The fragrance was sweet and Prescott remembered that fragrance from the days of his youth when he and his uncle would go fishing in the river. Two bird dogs—pointers— Mack and Moe—lounged by the fire and Prescott stroked their heads.

"How's your pa?" Verlon asked.

"All right."

"Your grandma comes over to see me sometimes. She gets one of your brothers to hitch up the buggy and she rides over all by herself. She's truly a remarkable woman."

"That she is. Can you imagine Grandpa and Grandma sneaking through the Yankee lines to get to Kingston?"

"It's a good thing the Yankees didn't catch them," Verlon said. "Grandma would have shot them."

"I thought you might have come over for Christmas dinner."

"No. I ain't much for family gatherings. Never have been. I know it must have been tough—your ma not being there this year."

"Yes, it was."

"Your ma was a fine woman, the finest I reckon I ever knew," Verlon said and he lowered his face.

The wood in the fireplace shifted position and the coals beneath the firedogs glowed a bright red. He looked around the room. Long cane fishing poles leaned against one corner. In another corner stood two shotguns.

"Did you go hunting yesterday?" Verlon asked.

"Yes. My brothers and I went. Pa doesn't go hunting anymore."

"I heard the guns. You must have had luck."

"I can't complain. It was a wonderful day to hunt. All the time I was in France I thought about those Christmas hunts. I hoped I'd make it home to do it again. Uncle Verlon, how've you been getting along?"

Verlon removed the pipe from his mouth and knocked the bowl into a tin peach can and emptied the dark tobacco. Then he removed a pouch from his coat and refilled the bowl and struck a match and lit it. He breathed deeply until the bowl was glowing red once again.

"I'm getting to be an old man, Pres. Not as quick on my feet anymore."

"You're not old."

Verlon grinned.

"Yeah, afraid so. Old enough. I read about you in the paper. Old Marcus devoted a lot of space to you. You acquitted yourself well, I'd say."

"I didn't think about it at the time."

"I don't suppose there's much time to think."

"There's time only to act and react. If you take time to think—well, sometimes, you don't come out of it alive."

The wind howled around the corner of the cabin and Prescott thought for a moment the walls were shaking. He preferred to think not of the winter days but the summer days of his youth when he and his uncle sat on the cool wood floor and sorted through the fishing tackle. Verlon was particular. He had to be sure he had so many hooks of different sizes and so many lead weights and so many cork floats. The interior of his cabin was usually in disarray but his tackle box was always in perfect order. Prescott remembered those days along the Etowah and Two-Run Creek when the heat was a smothering blanket and the water was cold and refreshing. He and his uncle fished until the fish stopped biting and then they swam in the cold current and let their bodies be swept along into the shallows. In those days Prescott heard about war, about the invasion, about all that was lost. It was difficult to imagine an enemy marching across the land that he called his own, an enemy that spoke the same language he spoke. In those days, those days of endless summer heat and trout and catfish, he never imagined himself in a war also. He simply sat and listened and the stories became a part of the fabric that he called Prescott Freeman.

Prescott studied his uncle. Verlon and Thaddeus had not spoken to each other in over twenty years. The wind rattled the shutters and Prescott rolled a cigarette and lit it and the two men sat and listened to the voice of winter and smoked. Then there was a pawing at the door and Verlon rose and opened it. Colonel, a bluetick hound, rushed in and shook himself in front of the fire and joined the two bird dogs. Verlon returned to the iron bed and sat.

"Colonel, what do you think about the snow?" Prescott asked and he ran his hand along the wet fur on the dog's back. "Can he still tree a possum?"

"You bet. He's still the best hunting dog in Bartow County. I'm just too slow to keep up with him now.

Anytime you want to take him out for some hunting, feel free to. He'd love the companionship of a young hunter."

"Thanks."

Verlon rubbed the gray stubble on his chin and then locked his left thumb inside one of his suspenders.

"Pres, you made us all proud when you got that law degree. What are you planning to do now? Or have you thought that far ahead?"

"I haven't decided. Pa wants me to go into one of the businesses."

Verlon bit down hard on the pipe, released the suspender and ran his left hand beneath his nose. He took a deep breath and studied his nephew.

"Is that what you want to do?"

"No, not really."

"It's none of my affair. But you belong on the land. Marry and settle down. You should see Preacher McIntosh's daughter."

"I have."

Verlon slapped his left knee.

"Isn't she something?"

"She is beautiful."

"That red hair—"

"She is beautiful, Uncle Verlon."

"Marry her and your father-in-law would be a preacher. That would put you closer to the man upstairs."

"Well, I'm not so sure about that. I've always been able to count on you for advice."

"Even when it's unsolicited. I have a little fun with the preacher, but he's a good man. A mighty fine umpire too. But just a plain good man. He comes to see me. He'll pull up a chair and talk for an hour or more. He's well educated but he don't put on no airs. I like talking to him. He refers to me as a voice in the wilderness. I kind of like the sound of that. He doesn't hit me with a lot of hellfire and brimstone. He's just not like that. But he cares about people. I think he's concerned about my soul. I guess I'm glad somebody is. "

"I'm concerned about your soul too. We all are."

"You can't say that with a straight face."

Prescott smiled and looked away.

"Uncle Verlon, there's a chance I may leave. I may not be able to stay here."

"Well, if you leave, I can't say I blame you. Too much is going on."

"I guess you're referring to—"

"That mess with Galen. Yeah, I know all about it. I suppose the whole town knows about it but your pa thinks he's keeping it quiet. He has his head in facts and figures. Sometimes he doesn't know what's going on around him. No, I shouldn't say that. I'm sorry, Pres. I shouldn't say anything against your pa—at least not in your presence. I'm sure he's doing what he thinks is right."

"I think he's wrong this time," Prescott said and he flipped the cigarette into the fireplace.

"Your pa is a hard man to reason with," Verlon said. "Morgan Ledbetter ain't no better. I've always said those two are going to kill themselves some day."

"I hope you're wrong. Uncle Verlon, you ever get lonesome living here all by yourself?"

"I'm not living here by myself. I've got Colonel and Mack and Moe. And they don't complain too much. When they do, I just ignore them."

Prescott glanced out the one window. The snow had almost stopped.

"There's a break in the snow. I'd better be going. I just wanted to say—"

"Hello, not good-bye. At least I sure hope it's not good-bye. Something tells me you're going to stay here. This land has a pull on you, stronger than the pull of the war you've just fought in. I know there's a whole other world out there, and you've seen a lot of it, a lot maybe you wish you hadn't seen. But this land is where you belong, Pres. I can see it. I hope you can."

"It's good to talk to you, Uncle Verlon. Take care."

"Don't mind me, Pres. You're the one who needs to take care."

Prescott walked outside and climbed on top of the mare. The wind was blowing the snow off the roof of the cabin and he backed the horse away and turned and left. The trees glistened in the grayness and the fields lay quiet in the whiteness. He looked over his shoulder one last time at the cabin.

The break in the snow did not last long. The flakes, large, white, beautiful, came down in a rush and they coated the countryside. Snow covered his coat and saddle. The mare was impervious. Prescott rode slowly and the old stories swirled like the snow-laden northwest wind in his mind. He had never heard the countryside so quiet. Not even a dog was barking. He rode through the Iron Hill community, past the small farms. He saw the McLaren place. A plow lay in the front yard, rusting. Thaddeus held the mortgage on the farm and all its equipment.

"Jeb McLaren isn't much of a farmer," Thaddeus said before Prescott left for war. "If he ends up losing the place, it's just as well. That's good land. It needs to be worked by someone who knows what he's doing."

Thaddeus did not know how to work the land himself, but he looked at land and saw the profit it could make. He never reached down and scooped up a handful of dirt and let it slide between his fingers. He did not know its feel. He did not know its smell. Prescott rolled another cigarette. The wind reddened his face but the cigarette somehow lessened the sting. The horse stepped through the snow and followed the road it knew so well.

Prescott came to a crossroads and brought the mare to a halt. Instead of continuing to the Hill, he urged the mare in the direction of town. The mare shook her head, confused, but obeyed. On the northern outskirts of town the houses were close together. Lights burned in the windows and the smell of firewood was good. It was like a moment from years ago. Everything seemed the same. But he was not the same. He knew it. Grandma Freeman suspected it. Thaddeus did not know. There was money to be made and Prescott could help him make it.

The Baptist church sat on a corner not far from the Methodist church and the Presbyterian church. Lights shone against the stained glass windows and he stopped at the hitching post. The church was brick, not large. The roof was steeply pitched. A white steeple sat securely on top.

One of the two front doors was open and Avanelle stood in the doorway. Twilight descended on the town but even in the dimness and the grayness her red hair shone brightly. He sat on the horse and she came to him. She wore no coat, no shawl. The snow clung to the green dress.

"I didn't think you were coming," she said.

"I didn't come for the interview."

"Why did you come?"

"You shouldn't be out here in the snow without a coat."

"I wouldn't be out here in the snow if you would come inside."

He had no answer. He dismounted and tied the reins to the post and followed her into the sanctuary. Candles and kerosene lamps burned and he removed his hat and touched the back of one of the wooden pews. The wood was smooth. He had sat here many times. He looked up at the wooden pulpit.

"The thing I like about your father's preaching is he doesn't do a whole lot of shouting," Prescott said.

"Jonathan Edwards didn't have to shout," she said.

She sat in a pew and he sat in the one across the aisle from her.

"It's been awhile since you were in a church," she said.

"Yes, except—"

"Except the church that was a hospital."

"Yes."

The snow had melted into her dress and she shivered. Prescott noticed. A shawl was draped across another pew and he brought it to her and wrapped it around her shoulders. She looked up and said nothing. Again he sat.

"The interview," he said. "I guess the reason I came was to say I can't be interviewed now. There are things I can't talk about."

"I understand."

"Do you?"

"Yes. You're going to have to give folks the opportunity to understand."

"I hadn't thought about it."

"You need to think about it. Don't put a wall up around yourself. Many of the others who have come back have done just that. They have built this wall around themselves and no one can draw near. I'm sorry. I shouldn't be saying these things. I hardly know you. I mean—I know you. But when I knew you before, we were much younger. And now we're grown and it seems I hardly know you. Does that make sense?"

"Yes. Don't apologize."

He gripped his hat tightly and stood.

"I must be going. Thank you."

"For what?"

"For understanding."

He walked toward the door and the candlelight flickered against the walls and stained glass windows. At the door he stopped and turned around.

"Prescott, if you need someone to talk to, I'm here," she said.

He put the dark hat on and walked into the cold.

Walton Young

CHAPTER TEN

Across the snow-covered fields Galen stumbled and watched. He did not think anyone would come after him. After all, no one had seen him leave. His grandmother lay in her bedroom and Thaddeus locked himself in his study. Thaddeus mumbled that he did not want to be disturbed. Then he slammed the door shut and the lock clicked. Galen knew that Thaddeus had accomplished what he had set out to do. He knew that his father had left early in the morning. He overheard Grandma and Mandy talking about it. And now he was locked in his study. Thaddeus had probably poured a bourbon and had toasted himself for his cleverness in the face of disaster. Yes, his father was clever. No man could beat him in a business deal. At least, no one ever had. And, to Thaddeus, all this was a business deal. Nothing more, nothing less.

The wind pushed against Galen but he kept walking through the snow, up one hill and then up another. When he reached the top of one of the hills, he stopped and looked at the tracks behind him. The snow was coming down heavy now and soon the tracks would be covered. That was good, he said to himself, and he continued his journey.

The wool cap was pulled low over his forehead and ears. Still, he heard music, organ music. It was coming from the Hurstwood place and he listened. At first he thought the wind was rustling strange sounds out of the woods but the hymn became more distinct. Then he heard old man Hurstwood's bass voice singing "Onward, Christian Soldiers." Galen stopped and listened. The music reminded him of Sunday mornings in the Baptist church. The Freemans always sat midway to the right, but Thaddeus seldom came. His mother made sure the children got to church on time. The Ledbetters sat in the back to the left— that is, the Ledbetters minus Morgan, who never came. Absence from church was perhaps the only thing the two men had in common. Galen remembered the Sunday more than a year ago when he saw Emma. He had known her all her life but he had never really seen her until that morning. There was something about the sunlight sprinkling through the stained glass windows and settling softly on her face. During the sermon he kept looking over his shoulder and she pretended not to notice but she did. She smiled.

After the service he found her beside the Ledbetter buggy. Her brothers were riding mules. Her mother was talking to some women outside the church door next to a cluster of red azaleas. Galen looked around. No one was watching. He offered his hand to help Emma up into the buggy. Near the buggy the white and pink dogwoods were in full bloom. Emma's hair was golden, like the spring sunshine, and her blue eyes sparkled playfully.

"My pa don't cotton none to Freemans," she said.

"I'm not wanting to take your pa to the carnival in Rome, so I don't care what your pa thinks."

"I bet you care what your pa thinks," she said and she gripped the reins tightly.

"Pa doesn't tell me what to do."

"Yeah, right."

"I hear they got a new freak show this year," Galen said. "You like freaks?"

"Honey, sometimes I think I live in a freak show."

"They got new magic tricks too."

"Is there a magic trick to get me out of this town? That's a disappearing act I'd like to see. You sure seem to know a lot about this fair."

"I read the posters."

"And you believe everything you read, I guess."

"Emma, it'll be fun."

"I've always been partial to a good fair."

"A fair's no good if you're not with the right man."

"You look like a boy, Galen Freeman. Are you telling me you're a man now?"

"I'm telling you, Emma, that I'm the right man."

Her brothers sat on their mules and stared at Galen. Suddenly the mother was behind him.

"Wasn't that a wonderful sermon?" he asked and he tipped his hat to Myrtle Ledbetter.

The next night he and Emma slipped away. She ran down the hill to the Etowah, where he had a buggy waiting. They stared at each other, then smiled, and jumped in. The carnival was set up along the banks of the Coosa River not far from the country club where Thaddeus was a member.

Men played golf there, he had been told. But not Thaddeus—he was too busy. The night was full of talk, laughter, the smell of food. Electric lights were strung over the midway. Galen and Emma looked at the lights above their heads and felt as if they were in another land, a faraway land where hatred and bitterness did not exist.

After the lights of the fair went dark, Galen took Emma's hand and they walked across the bridge that spanned the Coosa. Live oaks spread their new canopy of leaves over them. Her cotton dress was thin and he smelled the perfume that more than likely belonged to her mother. They stopped and listened to their breathing.

A Model T sped out of the gates of the Coosa Country Club and four young men, all wearing white straw hats, shouted and sang. The tires crunched the gravel and pebbles went flying.

"I wonder how many of them will go to the war," she said. "They ain't thinking about it now, but this time next year they may be dead. Oh, I shouldn't have said that. Your brother has gone. Galen, I'm—"

"It's all right. Pres is doing what he wants to do. He's living his adventure. But I don't want to talk about him."

The Coosa flowed smoothly. The clear water gleamed in the pale moonlight. Talk and a bit of laughter came from the fairgrounds and then there was quiet.

"The magic show wasn't much," she said. "I was hoping it would give me the trick to get out of this place."

"Why do you want to leave so much?"

"What's there for me in Kingston? Your family has money. You can do pretty much whatever you want. But the Ledbetters have never been blessed with money. The opportunities ain't there for a girl like me. I need to get to Atlanta."

He grabbed her and held her tightly.

"Maybe you'll find a reason to stay."

"Are you the reason, Galen Freeman?"

"Well, just maybe I am."

"If we do this, Galen, there's no turning back. You hear me?"

"I hear you. There's no turning back."

"No matter what my pa says or what your pa says. Do you understand?"

"I understand."

The snow was falling so heavily that he could hardly see the field in front of him. It was not that much farther. There was no turning back. The organ music was behind him now and the words to the hymn were a distant memory, locked somewhere in the sanctuary on a warm spring morning when his eyes told her that he loved her and that he did not care what the Freemans and the Ledbetters thought.

He was a man, he said to himself in the snow, and he laughed out loud. Tears trickled from his eyes and he wiped them before they froze on his skin. He climbed the last hill and stood in the snow and the wind and looked into the valley at the Ledbetter place. Smoke from the rock chimney danced slowly in the wind. The roof was completely white. He saw no one.

She was there, Galen told himself. The afternoon faded into twilight. Soon nightfall would be complete and he felt even colder. He sat on the top of the hill and tried not to think about the darkness and the wind and the cold. He remembered the spring night when he took Emma in his arms and they were no longer a Freeman and a Ledbetter. They became something else, a new being. There was no turning back and he had turned back. He had bowed before Thaddeus's will. *Please let it be spring again.* But there in the wasteland of snow spring seemed something far off, a memory, not to be experienced again. He wanted to reach out and touch it and at the same time feel the warmth of Emma's breath upon his cheek. Galen sat in the snow and stared at the shack and did not move.

CHAPTER ELEVEN

Prescott rode slowly up the Hill and the snow fell in the darkness of early evening. Lights glowed in the windows of every room in the house. Perhaps they would be having dinner and he realized he was hungry. He rode to the stables, where he removed the bridle, saddle, and saddle blanket. He brushed the mare and then fed her oats.

"I bet you're hungry, old girl, just like me," he said.

He noticed Henry's horse in one of the stalls. It would not be much longer till he and Mandy married. Prescott was certain of that. Outside the wind swept across the pasture and the snow flew into his face. He lowered his head and walked from the stables to the house. The entrance hall was quiet. All the voices were coming from the dining room.

"Well, it's about time you showed up," Sam said.

They were sitting at the table. Grandma Freeman looked worried. The lines in her forehead were deep. Thaddeus hardly looked up.

"Where's Galen?" William asked. "We thought he might be with you."

"No, he's not with me," Prescott said and he removed his coat and hung it on the halltree.

"Well, I wonder where he could be," Grandma Freeman said. "Thaddeus, did he say anything to you?"

"No, he said nothing to me," Thaddeus said and he sliced through the ham on his plate.

"Henry, how are you doing?" Prescott asked. "You're becoming a regular fixture around here."

Henry sat next to Mandy opposite Prescott.

"Pres, will you be ready to pitch in the spring?" Henry asked.

"I don't know. I haven't thought about it."

"Of course he'll be ready to pitch in the spring," William said. "Now that you're out of the army, you'll be ready, won't you, Pres?"

Prescott looked up from his plate. They were all staring at him.

"I mean—that Rome bunch swept us last year," Henry said. "They had a big old time. You should have seen them, Pres. Laughing, carrying on. We needed a pitcher who could sit them down at the plate. Man, I'm glad you're out of the army."

"Henry, there's no law that says you can't take up pitching yourself," Prescott said.

"It's true. There's no law, but there's bad eyesight. Even with these spectacles I'm not sure I could see the signs."

"Pres, you are out of the army, aren't you?" Mandy asked.

The family stopped eating. Even Thaddeus lowered his knife and fork and stared at his oldest son.

"Actually, I still am in the army," Prescott said. "I told them I would make a final decision by the first of the year."

"I figured you mustered out in France," William said.

"No big deal," Sam said. "You can muster out here. Maybe we can have a mustering out party."

"You are mustering out, aren't you?" Mandy asked.

"Yes, he's staying here," Thaddeus said. "Stop asking him these ridiculous questions. He's got a business head on his shoulders, unlike some of you."

"Merry Christmas to you, too," Grandma Freeman said. "Right now I'm concerned about Galen. This is no night to be out. Pres, where do you think he might be?"

"I really don't know, Grandma. After I eat, I'll go out looking for him."

"You'll do nothing of the sort," Thaddeus said. "Galen is a grown man. He knows how to take care of himself."

"He might be hurt," Mandy said. "It's terribly cold out there."

Thaddeus bit down hard on the ham. Mandy understood. She lowered her head. Prescott covered his plate with ham, mashed potatoes, turnip greens, and cornbread. The flames in the fireplace were dwindling and the room was growing cold. Outside the wind was still careening around the corners of the house. Grandma Freeman shivered.

"Sam, aren't you supposed to be in charge of the fire?" she asked.

"I'm sorry."

Sam jumped up from the table and lifted a large log from the log box and tossed it in the fireplace. Flames leaped and sparks and cinders scurried up the chimney. The coals grew hotter and warmth spread throughout the room.

"I've gotten word the government is going to get rid of some of the ships the navy has," Thaddeus said. "There may be an opportunity."

"Pa, you're not going into shipping, are you?" William asked.

"Maybe. Why not? Of course, we can always dismantle the ships and do something with the metal."

"That'd be a whole lot of metal, Pa," William said.

"So it would require a whole lot of imagination. Pres, that's where you come in. That's something you can look into."

Prescott raised the fork to his mouth but halted and then lowered it. He knew nothing about ships and scrap metal and had no desire to learn. He looked at the end of the table. His grandmother was observing him.

"Prescott would rather play baseball," Henry said.

"Henry, you're not a member of this family yet," Thaddeus said. "Until you are, business discussions are off limits."

"Pa, that's rude," Mandy said.

"Your father is just being your father," Grandma Freeman said. "Henry, your opinions are always welcome."

"Thank you, Mrs. Freeman."

Prescott finished his dinner but remained at the table. The others, except his grandmother, rose and went down the hall to the living room. The flames in the fireplace rose even higher. He lifted his cup of coffee and drank and listened. The door to his father's study closed. In the parlor piano music began. Mandy was playing for Henry.

"I should go look for Galen," Prescott said.

"No, your father is probably right. Galen is a grown man. He will be fine. Never mind me. I'm just an old woman who worries too much about her grandbabies. Besides, where would you look? He could be anywhere. Or he might not be here at all. He might have gotten on board the southbound."

Prescott nodded his head and drank more coffee. Then he reached into his shirt pocket for tobacco and paper.

"Your mother never wanted you to smoke," Grandma Freeman said.

"She never wanted me to kill people either."

He rolled the cigarette and struck a match on the underside of the table. He inhaled deeply and sent a ring of smoke into the air.

"Pres, please stay," Grandma Freeman said. "I realize it's hard to stay on a farm after you've seen a lot of the world. But this is who you are."

"What about Grandpa? "

"It was always difficult to keep your grandfather here on the farm. I mean, he loved it here on the Hill. No question about it. In the mornings, especially in the spring, he'd walk out on the porch and take a deep breath and smile the biggest smile you've even seen. But those spring mornings weren't enough. He'd have to travel—to Atlanta, even to Washington. And, of course, there was that trip out West. He traveled mighty far to kill a man. When I looked at your grandfather, I never could envision someone who had killed. When I look at you, I feel the same way."

He lowered his head. He started to lift the cup but he returned it to the saucer.

"There was always something pulling at your grandfather to take him away," she said. "And there was always something pulling at him to bring him back here. That something was the land, and it's pulling you back. I know it is. Pres, listen to it. Listen to what it has to say to you."

Prescott looked up at the ceiling and took a deep breath.

"I do love this place. When I was in France, I thought about it so much—when there was time to think."

The piano grew quiet. There was only the sound of the fire. He looked at the flames. Streaks of blue mixed with the red.

"Tell me about your girl," Grandma Freeman said.

"What makes you think—"

"Oh, you can't fool me, Prescott Freeman. No Freeman has ever fooled me. Your grandfather thought he could but he was wrong. I've known since shortly after you came back. I just wanted to wait about asking until the others weren't around. Now tell me about her. For starters—what is her name?"

"Natasha."

"Natasha. What a beautiful name. It sounds—"

"Russian."

"Where did you meet her?"

"In Paris. Her family had emigrated there."

"Where is she now? You should have brought her home for Christmas."

"She is in Russia."

"I don't understand," Grandma Freeman said. "You said her family had moved to Paris. And Natasha is in Russia? I don't understand."

"I've been in Russia also."

In her faded blue eyes there was a look of deepening concern.

"But there's revolution, civil war in Russia. You survived the war in France. The army should not have put you in such danger again."

"It was my decision, Grandma."

"I don't understand, Pres. I'm an old woman and some things are hard for me to get a good grasp of. And this is one of those things. Do you love this girl? Why is she still in Russia?

"I had to leave her in Russia. Grandma, I appreciate your wanting to know about her, but I can't talk about it. Someday, perhaps. But not tonight."

Outside a shrill call erupted. A chill shot through the room. The screech owl shrieked once and was gone.

CHAPTER TWELVE

In the dim yellow light of a kerosene lamp Emma writhed on the bed. Her head turned quickly from side to side and her mother sat beside her and lay the cold wet cloth on her hot forehead. Morgan Ledbetter stood in the darkness, implacable, unyielding. Behind him his sons sat at the table, afraid. With each moan and then with each scream their eyes looked on with terror, not knowing what to do. They sat and waited for Ledbetter to say something. Myrtle rose and went to Morgan.

"You'd better send one of the boys to get the doc," she said.

"Is it time? I didn't think the baby was due this soon."

"You got eyes, don't you? Babies come when they get good and ready to come."

"Could be something she ate."

"Morgan, if you don't get help for that girl, you'll live the rest of your life in damnation. You hear me? Look at her. Our girl is dying, and you ain't got sense enough to see it."

Morgan pushed Myrtle aside and stepped into the room and looked down on his daughter. Her face was flushed and she shivered. He reached down and pulled the quilt over her. She opened her eyes and did not see him. She looked at the blackness beyond the window.

"Galen, Galen!"

Myrtle rushed to her side.

"What is it, honey?"

"Galen, Galen! It's Galen, Mama."

"No, honey. Galen isn't here."

"Yes, Mama, it's Galen. I know it. I saw him. Oh, Mama! I knew he would come! Open the door and let him in!"

Emma moaned and Myrtle rose furiously into Morgan's face.

"Send for the doc. And send for that preacher fellow, McIntosh. He's a good man. We need him."

"He's close to the Freemans. I don't want their preacher here at a time like this. I ain't going to send for him."

"If'n you don't, I'll go myself. You hear me, Morgan Ledbetter?"

He wrapped his thumbs around the strap of his overalls and he turned and walked into the other room where his sons waited and wondered.

"Josiah, I want you to go fetch the doc," Morgan said.

"Pa, is Emma—is she—I mean—is she going—to—"

"Don't ask any of your foolish questions. I don't want to hear them. Your ma says Emma needs the doc, so go find him. Don't come back without him. You understand?"

Josiah nodded.

"Stephen, you know where that Baptist preacher fellow lives?"

"Yes, Pa."

"Go get him."

Josiah and Stephen stood and put on their coats. They left and slammed the door quickly to keep out the wind. Morgan returned to Emma's bedside. Myrtle wiped the perspiration from Emma's forehead. Suddenly Emma pushed herself up by her elbows.

"Galen, Galen!" Emma shrieked.

Myrtle grabbed her shoulders and eased her back onto the bed.

"Lay back down now, honey," the mother said. "Don't be stirring any."

Emma stared at the window and smiled. Ledbetter grew scared. He could not show it. He would not let any of them know it, but he was scared. It was the smile that scared him. It was a strange smile, a smile not of this world.

"It's Galen. He's come for me. I told you he would."

"Yes, honey."

"He loves me. He loves the baby."

Myrtle began to cry and Morgan looked away.

"Thaddeus Freeman is a scourge upon this land," he said. "He has taken what is mine and he will pay. If this here girl dies, as the Lord God Almighty is my witness, I'm going to kill him!"

"Shut your mouth, Morgan," Myrtle said.

"I wasn't speaking to you."

"I heard you. And I ain't going to stand for that kind of talk, not when my baby is lying here out of her head, seeing things that ain't there. Maybe it would ease her if Galen was here. Maybe we should go get him. I think he'd want to know."

"No!" Morgan said. "Woman, I've listened to your sass all night. You've told me what to do and I've done it. But there I draw the line. No Freeman enters that door. If he does, it'll be the last door he ever walks through!"

His whole body trembled in the dim lamplight.

VERLON STOOD ON THE NARROW PORCH and drew deep puffs on the pipe. The wind whistled through the clusters of oaks and hickories. Pines swayed and the branches sagged with the weight of the snow. The hound sat at his feet as if waiting to go on a hunt. Verlon admired the white blanket that stretched from the steps to the edge of the forest. This kind of snow did not come often but when it did come, it was nice, something to admire. The bird dogs enjoyed it. They romped in the yard but Colonel remained on the porch next to Verlon's boots. Deep within the woods a screech owl cried and the bird dogs ran onto the porch and Verlon cringed.

"Boys, that's a sound I hate to hear. What about you fellows? If I knew where that old screech owl was, I'd get my gun and we'd go kill it. Well, we don't know, so we'd best be getting' back inside. It gives me the jitters."

They went into the cabin and he sat on the edge of the bed. He had left the door of the stove open and the red glow of the fire lit up the room. The dogs curled up on dingy, torn blankets not far from the stove. Verlon refilled the bowl of the pipe and struck a match on the sole of his boot. It was good of Prescott to come visiting. Thaddeus would have objected but one good thing about Prescott was that he did what he wanted to do no matter what Thaddeus thought. Verlon grinned. Thaddeus wanted to control everyone. He could not control Prescott.

He puffed on the pipe and thought how good it was to sit in a cabin on a snowy night and listen to the stillness. But he was alone. Prescott asked him if it ever bothered him—his being alone. Well, sometimes it did. He did not talk about it. Little did he think about it. But here on this night with the blanket of snow outside his door and the wind rattling the shutters he wondered what it would be like to have a woman sitting in the rocking chair next to the stove, glasses sitting on the end of her nose, knitting something, perhaps a sweater. He stared at the rocking chair and envisioned it going back and forth, back and forth. He saw Abigail sitting in the chair, contented, and he felt that all was right in the world. But then the chair was empty and he felt the loneliness. If things had turned out differently. . . . Well, it was too late, years too late, a lifetime too late to speculate on what might have been. Still, he sat on the edge of the bed and stared at the vacant chair and wondered.

Prescott was not alone. He had plenty of family surrounding him, yet he seemed alone. Something was bothering the boy. Verlon had known him all his life. He had taught him how to hunt and how to fish. He had taught him to get close to nature, to kneel deep within the forest and listen to the voices coming from the trees and the springs and rivers and lakes, the voices of their ancestors who had come to this land and cleared it and made homes and raised families and tended and cared for the land. He had taught Prescott all these things, lessons Thaddeus could never teach because he never learned them himself. Verlon knew Prescott as if he were his son and he knew that he was deeply troubled. Well, he had been through a lot. He had been shot at. Verlon thought about his own father. He went through the crucible of war and did not emerge unscathed. Soldiers never did. Verlon looked at Prescott and saw his own father. Men had tried to kill Prescott. And he had killed. Verlon did not know how many. It was not really important whether it was one or a dozen. From the trench-infested, gas-plagued battlefields Prescott had come back different. The voice was different. The eyes were different. They had seen horrors other men could not imagine. It would take time for him to talk. Perhaps he never would. That was the way it was with the soldiers Verlon had known. Their eyes conveyed the hell through which they had walked, but they could not talk about it. One thing was certain—he would not be able to talk to Thaddeus. Thaddeus was too busy with finance. It was time for things to return to normal. There was money to be made. The war was simply an inconvenience.

Verlon wondered what his brother looked like these days. When he was in the general store or the barbershop, he heard other men talk about Thaddeus. He heard that his brother was stooped over a bit—no doubt the result of sitting hunched over all those financial books, credits and debits, debits and credits. Thaddeus must have been around when the first dollar was minted. He and money had a special kinship. Well, he could not sit here and fault him for making money. It must be a gift and Thaddeus knew how to develop it. But profits came with a steep price, and Thaddeus had not paid it. Other folks had.

THE OCTOBER SUN DIPPED BEHIND the crest of the hill that overlooked the Etowah. The late afternoon chill settled in the valley of the Etowah but Verlon did not notice. All he thought about was Abigail. He had shed his overalls and put on dark trousers and a clean white shirt. He walked quickly along the dusty road—the fall was especially dry that year and dust hung in the air and burned a red sheen onto the countryside—that climbed the hill where their tree overlooked the river. It had been their tree for many years. It was an oak, big and full, and the leaves were beginning to turn. But it had been so dry that the leaves were simply turning to brown. He had climbed the tree as a boy. Abigail never would.

"You be careful, Verlon Freeman," she had said.

She would look up at him and shake her head.

"Come on up."

"I'm not climbing that tree. And you shouldn't either. You'll fall."

"I ain't never fallen, have I?"

"There's a first time, ain't there?"

By the time he reached the crest of the hill twilight was spreading across the valley and in the western sky thin clouds were a deep orange. The Etowah flowed dark beneath him. He saw her at the foot of the tree. Her cotton dress flowed freely and her dark brown hair was pulled straight back and balled at the back of her head. She was not alone. Verlon drew closer and stopped. Thaddeus came out of the shadows and confronted him. Even in those days Thaddeus nearly always wore a suit. He worked little on the farm. His interests lay elsewhere.

"Hello, brother," Thaddeus said.

"What are you doing here?"

Abigail looked feverishly from Thaddeus to Verlon and then back to Thaddeus. A whippoorwill sang its lonely song from the forests and Verlon grew anxious.

"I'll make it short, Verlon," Thaddeus said. "Abigail and I are going to be married."

Verlon looked sharply at Abigail but she avoided his eyes. He could tell she had been crying. Her eyes were still red and her hands trembled. Verlon did not understand. The man standing before him was his brother but he did not know him.

"Married? Are you crazy? What's he talking about, Abigail?"

"I'm doing the talking, Verlon," Thaddeus said.

"You can do the talking when I ask you a question. Abigail, what's all this about?"

She lowered and shook her head. The tears came again and she wiped them. Thaddeus put his hands on his hips. It seemed he was impatient. He did not have time for this.

"There's nothing much I can say," she said.

Verlon brushed past Thaddeus and walked up to Abigail. Still, she kept her head lowered. He touched her chin and moved her face toward his. In a field on the other side of the river doves were cooing the end of the day. Thaddeus turned and stood beside Abigail. Verlon raised his hand and pointed at the heart, awkwardly carved in the bark of the oak. In the darkness it was hardly visible. He pointed to the VF + AS.

"You remember that, Abigail? Do you remember that day? Abigail, you and I made promises that day. We mapped out our future. We knew exactly what we wanted in this world."

"That's what children do," Thaddeus said. "Abigail is a grown woman."

"Abigail, I'm speaking to you," Verlon said. "Please— answer me. Don't you remember that day—all our hopes we talked about, right here, beneath this tree. Don't you remember?"

The young woman looked away. Verlon touched her arm. She wore no sweater or shawl and her arm was cold. The sky lost its orange and a sliver of moon drooped lazily. At the foot of the hill the Etowah sloshed and scurried past them on its way to the foothills. Verlon's hand climbed up her arm to her shoulder and she cried.

"Abigail, won't you talk to me?" Verlon asked. "Sweetheart, I'm begging you. This is like some kind of nightmare. I never expected something like this. Tell me this is not happening."

"I can't," she said. "I'm going to marry Thaddeus."

"But you don't love him."

"Of course she does," Thaddeus said. "Verlon, there's something you just don't understand. You never have. You never will. Abigail wants a man who's going to amount to something, somebody who doesn't spend every spare minute off in the woods hunting or fishing. Haven't you heard? We're living in the age of business. There's money to be made—a lot of money—but, Verlon, you have to work to get it. Chasing a quail or a catfish isn't going to put money in your pocket. Like I said, you don't understand. I understand and Abigail understands. She wants to marry a man with a business head on his shoulders."

"You don't love him, Abigail. I haven't heard you say you love him. If you did, you would say it."

"All right. I love him. There. I said it."

Thaddeus smiled.

"Don't take it so hard," Thaddeus said.

Verlon's balled fist flew through the air and Thaddeus lay on the ground. Abigail screamed and Thaddeus sat up and wiped the blood from his nose on his coat sleeve. Abigail rushed between them. Tears streaked down her face. Verlon stared at her and then turned and walked away.

"Verlon! Verlon!"

Verlon walked down the hill and Abigail's voice followed him until it grew faint and disappeared. He walked across the cotton field which had been picked clean. Promises, he kept saying to himself. Promises.

VERLON TOSSED A CHUNK OF WOOD into the stove and rubbed his hands in front of the fire. Such a long time ago, he said to himself. He did not really blame Abigail though for a long time he did. Her family had little. The war pretty much wiped their plow clean. They even had to sell off most of their land and they struggled to keep what little they had left. She needed a husband who would provide. And Thaddeus provided. He gave her things he himself could not. The anger had left long ago. And now she was gone. It was hard to believe. For many years he had climbed the hills and looked in the direction of her house. Sometimes if the wind was blowing just right, the smoke from the chimneys cleared the treetops and he could see it and he could imagine her inside the house. And now she was gone. Despite the anger, despite the hurt, despite the struggle to understand, just knowing she was on the other side of the valley was a comfort. And now she was gone. Thaddeus took it hard. Friends had told him. But he took it hard as well. With her passing a part of him was gone forever. He never stopped loving her.

Colonel raised his head. The bird dogs grew tense.

"What is it, boys?"

The dogs growled and stood in front of the door. Verlon went to the corner and lifted the 12-gauge and stepped onto the porch. It was perhaps a fox or even a panther that had come down out of the mountains. He had heard the stories all his life. The cries of the screech owl were a harbinger of death and sometimes a panther would come down and cry. He saw no fox. He saw no panther. The dark figure of a man trudged through the snow and stopped a dozen feet from the steps. The snow was deep and the man was breathing heavily.

"Uncle Verlon."

"Galen?"

"Yeah, it's me."

"My God, boy, come in and get warm."

Galen left his tracks in the snow, but they were quickly covered. The dogs recognized Galen, wagged their tails in greeting and returned to their blankets and Galen stood in front of the stove. His hat and coat dripped water onto the floor, where it puddled at his wet boots. He shivered.

"Thanks for letting me in," Galen said.

"You should thank me for not shooting you. I thought you might be a panther. I've been hearing that old screech owl and I'm a bit jumpy. What are you doing out in this mess at this time of night?"

"She's dead, Verlon."

"Dead? Is Ma—"

"I waited. I saw the doctor and the preacher go in. She's dead. What kind of man am I? I just sat and waited while she died."

"Galen, what are you talking about? Is Ma—?"

"I should have been there with her and I was too much of a coward. I'm all hollow inside, Uncle Verlon. She's dead. There's nothing in the world for me. Nothing."

CHAPTER THIRTEEN

Avanelle lifted the pot of hot water from the wood-burning stove and poured it into the sink. Her mother washed the supper dishes and Avanelle dried them. Her father sat in his study working on the Sunday sermon. The wind had died and there was a quiet that bothered her.

Elizabeth McIntosh was a large woman, a strong woman. Everything about her suggested strength—especially her hands and her eyes. She too had red hair but it was streaked with gray. The lines in her face had deepened. Her green eyes had lost the vibrancy that shone in Avanelle's. She had ridden in the buggy with her husband on missions to comfort, to uplift, to encourage in times of death and despair. She had been with him after births and funerals. She had seen joy and she had seen sorrow. She was not good with words, she always said, but Caleb McIntosh did not believe it. It was not so much the words themselves, but the tone and the touch of her hand that soothed the grieving.

"It's so quiet," Avanelle said.

She took the plates she had dried to the pie safe and stacked them carefully.

"Sometimes it's like that in a storm," her mother said. "It's like the wind just finally blows itself out and stops for a while. But it can fool you. It can start up in a hurry."

"It was snowing when little Johnny died."

Elizabeth nodded. The baby was only six days old.

"Yes. I'm surprised you remember."

"I remember."

"Your father told me you saw Pres Freeman today."

"Yes. We saw him at the newspaper. Then he came by the church. I was hoping to get an interview."

"Did you?"

"No. He said he wasn't ready to talk about the war."

"Give him time."

"I think it's going to take a lot of time," Avanelle said.

"Perhaps it will. You know, it wasn't too long ago, before he left for the war, when you talked about him quite a bit."

"Did I? I don't remember."

"You don't?"

"Well, maybe a little. I was young."

"You're still young. What was your impression of him today?"

"Oh, he's still the most handsome man. There's no denying that. He's intelligent. But there's a sadness in his eyes, Mother. I've never seen anything like it. It's like he sees things that only he can see. And the things he sees are full of sorrow."

Elizabeth stopped washing dishes for a moment and stared into the darkness outside the window. Slivers of light from the kitchen spilled onto the snow. The snow was beautiful and she remembered playing in the snow as a child. Her father was there but he did not smile. He did not laugh.

"When my father came home from the war," Elizabeth said, "it was as if a glaze hung over his eyes. He saw things, yet he didn't see them. At night he would wake up from his nightmares. He would be screaming and shaking and my mother and I and my brothers and sisters would try to calm him. I remember he would be shaking and sweating even if it was winter. My brothers and sisters and I were scared. Our daddy was gone a long time. We missed him so much. And then when he finally came home, limping, it was almost as if he wasn't our daddy at all. He was so different. He brought the nightmare of war home with him, and it never left. Gettysburg did that to a man. I suppose the Argonne did the same thing."

Elizabeth returned to the dishes and Avanelle remembered hearing about Prescott's leaving for the war. She wanted to say something to him. She wanted to tell him how brave she thought he was. She wanted to tell him to come home safely. But he left and she did not say those things. The horrors of 1918 came and she worried that something might happen to him. She went into the newspaper office each day to check the reports of casualties. She feared she would see his name and she said a prayer of thanksgiving each time she did not. And then she heard about his heroism in the Argonne. It seemed it was all the people of Kingston talked about—except those people whose sons and brothers and fathers were killed. Those people did not talk. But the others did. Jeffrey Freeman had been another hero in another war, and now there was Prescott.

She remembered his standing outside the church today, reluctant to come inside. She hated war. She wished he had never gone. So he was a hero. He had paid a price, apparently a terrible price, and she wondered what price would have to be paid to free him from the memories that clouded his eyes.

Suddenly someone pounded on the front door. Even in the kitchen the knock was loud. Avanelle and her mother looked at each other, left the sink and hurried down the hall past the parlor to the front door. McIntosh left his study across from the parlor and followed them. Avanelle opened the door and the coldness of the night air struck her bitterly. On the porch, a woolen cap in his hands, stood Stephen Ledbetter.

"Stephen, come inside," McIntosh said. "What brings you out in all this snow? Is everything all right?"

Stephen stepped into the entrance hall but did not look into their eyes. He was nervous, afraid.

"It's Emma."

"What's happening, Stephen?" Elizabeth said. "Is Emma all right?"

"No, ma'am. She ain't doing too well. Josiah has gone to fetch Doc Evans. Pa sent me to get you, Preacher. I'm scared. I'm scared she ain't going to make it."

"I'll harness the buggy," McIntosh said. "Are you on foot?"

"No, sir. I rode the mule."

McIntosh harnessed the buggy and picked up his wife and daughter at the front steps. Stephen was already on his way back. The preacher urged his horse onward into the snow, into the night. In the darkness the snow cast a brightness and Avanelle did not think she had ever seen anything so beautiful. They rode past forests with limbs bowing, almost touching the ground. They rode past pastures where the snow seemed to go on forever.

"It must be bad," Elizabeth said. "Avanelle and I saw her today and she didn't look well at all."

"Yes, I'm concerned. I wonder if anyone has gotten in touch with Galen."

"If Ledbetter sees Galen on his place, he'll probably kill him," Elizabeth said.

Avanelle and her mother huddled close together beneath a blanket. The wind stirred for only a moment and then subsided. Dogs barked from their porches and occasionally a farmer would step out of his house and strain to see who was traveling. Only one seemed to recognize them.

"Well, howdy, Preacher! Where you heading?"

McIntosh did not answer. The snow was deep but he urged the horse to go faster. Avanelle stared at the snow and thought about what might be waiting for them.

When they arrived at the Ledbetters, Doc Evans's horse was tied to the hitching post. McIntosh tied his horse and helped Elizabeth and Avanelle onto the steps.

"Be careful," he said. "They're slick."

They shook the snow from their coats and stomped their boots and shoes on the porch, knocked and went in. Morgan sat in the split-bottom chair next to the fireplace and did not look up. Josiah and Stephen were at the table; their heads rested in their hands. Doc Evans pulled back the curtain. He was an old, thin man with a short white beard. Except for the years he spent in medical training, he had lived his whole life in Kingston. He had brought Emma into the world seventeen years ago. He had delivered her brothers as well.

"They told me you were coming," Doc Evans said. "I'm glad you're here. Elizabeth, I'm going to need your help and yours too, Avanelle. I need hot water and towels."

Josiah grabbed a bucket from the dry sink and rushed outside to the well. Stephen put more wood in the stove and Josiah returned and set the bucket on top of the stove. Elizabeth found some towels inside the dry sink and waited for the water to heat.

McIntosh walked over to Ledbetter. Still he did not look up.

"Morgan, is there anything I can do for you?"

"She's going to die. I know it just as sure as I'm sitting here."

"Doc Evans is a good man," McIntosh said. "Do you want me to pray?"

"No. Prayers won't do no good, not now. Just let me be, Preacher."

McIntosh sat on the bed and waited. Josiah lifted the bucket and carried it past the curtain. Avanelle and her mother followed. In the air was the odor of fresh blood. Myrtle kneeled on the far side of the bed and clutched her daughter's hand. She was weeping. Avanelle looked at Emma. She was motionless. Her face was a deathly white. Doc Evans pulled back the blanket. Bright red blood soaked the sheet.

"We've got to hurry."

Josiah walked out and leaned against the wall near his father. Ledbetter did not want to hear a prayer, but McIntosh closed his eyes and prayed.

The clock on the mantel ticked slowly, so slowly that time seemed to stop. And then there was the cry—the cry of a newborn. Ledbetter and his sons looked up. On their faces there was hope. In their eyes was the hope that in their wasteland of despair something good was going to happen. And then there was the cry—the cry of a woman pouring out the grief that had built up inside her.

Doc Evans walked past the curtain and faced Ledbetter. His white shirt was covered with blood. He was tired. His knees were about to buckle.

"You've got a grandson," Doc Evans said. "He's a fine healthy baby boy."

"And Emma?" Ledbetter said.

The doctor looked down and slowly shook his head. He had spent his adult life giving good news and bad news. The bad never came easily. He looked up and stared at Ledbetter.

"I'm sorry, Morgan. She didn't make it. The baby was turned sideways and there was a hemorrhage. We did everything we could, but she just lost too much blood. If we could have gotten her to the hospital earlier—"

"If! I don't want to hear nothing about 'if'!"

McIntosh stood but Ledbetter's face told him to come no closer. Elizabeth walked into the room. She carried the baby in a white blanket and fought back the tears that wanted to stream down her face. Behind her Myrtle wept.

"Morgan, here is your grandson," she said.

"Don't bring him to me. I don't want to see him. He's got Freeman blood in him."

"Morgan, he's got Ledbetter blood in him too," McIntosh said. "He's your grandson."

"Your wife needs you," Elizabeth said.

"Let me be, woman."

Elizabeth cuddled the newborn and looked at Josiah.

"We're going to need milk," she said. "Josiah, did you hear me? We're going to need milk."

Josiah grabbed the pail near the stove and walked outside toward the barn. He wore no coat, yet he did not feel the cold. Suddenly he stopped before the dark figure behind McIntosh's buggy.

"Josiah, how is she?"

"How could you come—now? Where were you? She called for you—right up until the moment she died."

Josiah dropped the pail and grabbed Galen by the coat collar.

"I could kill you! Right now I could kill you!"

Josiah flung Galen to the snow and wiped the tears.

"She's dead?"

"Yes, she's dead. Because of you, she's dead. You'd better get out of here. Any moment now Pa is going to come out that door and if he sees you, he won't just talk about killing you. He will kill you, Galen Freeman. So leave—now—and never come back."

Galen struggled to his feet and backed away. Inside a woman was crying bitterly. He walked away from the shack and when he was a mile down the snow-covered road, he realized he had not asked about the baby.

CHAPTER FOURTEEN

Prescott climbed the back stairs slowly. His leg ached in the coldness. Down the hall music and laughter erupted again. Mandy and Henry were at the piano. They played and sang Cohen, and Prescott wished he could smile. In the darkness at the top of the stairs he heard the voices, but they were not the voices from downstairs. They were voices from far away in a land that seemed to know no warmth.

He opened the door to his room and walked inside. The coals in the fireplace had lost their red glow. His wool topcoat lay on the bed and he put it on and sat in the cane-bottom chair next to the window. Outside the land was white. The snow still came down and he closed his eyes and felt the cold wetness on his face. He opened and closed his hand and felt the grip of Natasha's small hand.

In the darkly lit dining room of the small hotel they sat at the long table and listened to the voices, the voices of her countrymen who had traveled far. Prescott listened but did not comprehend. He wished they would speak in French. Apparently they did not want him to know their thoughts. Natasha listened patiently and turned to him.

"They do not understand why we want to see General Graves," she said.

"I don't care what they don't understand," Prescott said.

"Dearest, do you really want me to tell them that?"

Prescott studied each face. The men were young, inexperienced. Only a few had beards. He looked into their eyes. They did not trust him. They did not trust any American. He was certain of that. There were only twenty. Forty to fifty had said in Paris they wanted to return to their homeland, but only twenty came. Twenty would certainly make a lot of difference.

"Pres, I'm really worried," Harry Truman said at the train depot. "These men know nothing of war."

"I guess that's why they need me."

"And what's more—Natasha knows nothing of war. This is her idea, and it's crazy. She's beautiful. I know how you feel about her. But she's going to get you killed. Because of a beautiful Russian princess, you're going to get killed."

"Take care, Harry."

The woman who ran the hotel—Prescott was not sure whether she owned it—brought more coffee and poured. She was a large woman whose dress was as dingy and shabby as the walls of the dining room. He looked at her face. She had seen many hard times, and she did not like these guests, including him. She was suspicious. She poured coffee into Natasha's cup and scowled and mumbled. She disappeared into the kitchen.

"I don't think she likes us," Prescott said.

"She will like us better when we help Kolchak defeat the Reds."

"Maybe she doesn't want the Reds defeated."

"What do I tell my fellow patriots? They do not want us to meet with General Graves. They want to go directly to Kolchak."

"Tell them my orders are to meet with the general. I intend to follow my orders. General Graves can arrange safe passage for us. If they don't like it, they can go on their own. You and I are leaving now to see him."

She spoke quickly and the men shook their heads and squirmed in their chairs. Prescott grabbed her arm and pulled her to her feet. They left the coffee and the men and the hotel and stepped into the deserted, snow-covered street. The night wind was bitterly cold and they had difficulty breathing. He put his arm around her and they walked toward the army compound.

"Is it far?" she asked.

"No."

The buildings of Vladivostok were low, no more than two stories, closely packed together, and the steeply sloped roofs were weighted down by the snow. There were no lights in the shop windows. The gas street lamps shone yellow and Prescott and Natasha walked in the middle of the street where the snow had been partially shoveled away into dunes in front of the shops. He stared at the darkened windows and felt as if hundreds of eyes were staring at them.

"It is not Paris, love," she said. "Nor is it Moscow. You really should see Moscow or St. Petersburg. I must take you when it is safe."

He wondered about the safety of the street before them but he said nothing. He did not like the woman at the hotel. The snow came down in swirls.

"Do you not like the snow?" she asked.

"I prefer the warmth and sunshine of the spring."

"That is when you play—what is the game?"

"Baseball."

"And you play a position of—"

"I'm the pitcher."

"Is that important?"

"Sort of."

"After the Bolsheviks are defeated, I will come to America and watch you play the position of pitcher. I will see how important it is."

Suddenly dogs growled and barked and Prescott and Natasha confronted a tall wire fence with guards carrying rifles and black-and-tan German Shepherds posted at the front gate. Beyond the fence large, low barracks-style buildings were barely visible. Smoke rose from the chimneys. A young soldier, a corporal, approached and, upon seeing the twin silver bars, stopped and saluted.

"Good evening, Corporal," Prescott said and answered the salute. "I am Captain Freeman. We're here to see General Graves."

"Yes, sir."

The corporal returned to the guard station and picked up the telephone. In a moment other guards pulled the wire gate open and Prescott and Natasha entered the compound.

"Please follow me, Captain," the corporal said.

Unlike the downtown street, dim lights shone through the windows of the buildings. From some buildings talking and laughter escaped into the night. Ice cracked loudly beneath their boots. The compound was large, larger than

Prescott had expected, large enough to house nine thousand troops.

The corporal led them down what appeared to be several alleys to a building that was three stories. Lights burned in only a few of the upstairs windows. An officer stood outside the door.

"Corporal, I'll take over from here," the officer said and he extended his hand. "Captain Freeman, I'm Major Clinton Jones."

"Major, this is Natasha Kamarov."

"Miss Kamarov, my pleasure."

"Major."

"General Graves is expecting you."

The major was probably in his forties, and Prescott wondered whether he had seen action in France. The first level of the building was cold and dark. It appeared to be used mostly for storage. Crates and boxes were stacked almost to the low ceiling. Jones walked briskly and Prescott smelled the stale dust that clung to the boxes and to the floor.

"We don't have an elevator," Jones said. "I hope you don't mind taking the stairs to the third floor."

They climbed the stairs and on the third floor a series of offices branched off from a main corridor. Most of the offices were dark but Prescott saw small wood desks and more boxes stacked against walls. They came to an anteroom and Jones asked them to wait and then he disappeared into another office. After only a moment he returned and they entered the office.

Major General William Graves rose from the chair behind his large desk and greeted Prescott and Natasha with a smile and handshake. He was a tall man, perfectly straight. Hair receded from his forehead and thin-rimmed spectacles perched on the end of his long slender nose. His thin mustache was neatly trimmed. He chose his words carefully. His voice was clipped, precise. He carried the type of military demeanor that Prescott had come to expect in high-ranking officers.

"Captain Freeman, Miss Kamarov, please have a seat," Graves said and he motioned them to the two chairs in front of the desk.

Jones turned and left and closed the door. Only a few papers dotted the top of the desk. Several bookcases lined the walls. Behind the desk a window overlooked the compound.

"General, thank you for meeting with us," Prescott said.

"My pleasure. I trust you find your accommodations satisfactory."

"Yes, General, very much so," Natasha said.

Prescott reached inside his topcoat pocket and withdrew an envelope and handed it to the general. Graves opened it and examined the paper in the dim light and then returned it to Prescott.

"Yes, this is the information I've already received," Graves said. "Miss Kamarov, do you mind if I smoke?"

"It is perfectly all right."

"Prescott, will you join me?"

"Yes, thank you, sir."

Graves handed a cigar box to Prescott and the two men struck matches.

"There is nothing like a good cigar," Graves said. "Prescott, would you agree?"

"Yes, sir."

"Especially when you're facing a difficult situation. I find that a good cigar helps me to concentrate."

"Is there a difficult situation?" Natasha asked.

"I understand twenty people have accompanied you," Graves said.

"That is correct," Natasha answered.

"That is quite a liberating force."

"It is a start."

"Of what?"

"Of—as you said—liberation."

"But whom are you liberating?"

Natasha did not answer. She did not like the questions. It appeared the general was setting some sort of a trap and she was not prepared. She studied Graves carefully.

"When can we meet with Kolchak?" she asked.

"What do you know about Alexandr Kolchak?" Graves said.

"He's our leader against the Bolsheviks. He is fearless. He will not be defeated. He will drive Lenin and his crowd from power."

"How about you, Prescott? What do you know about Kolchak?"

"Not very much, sir."

"Miss Kamarov, have you ever met Kolchak?"

"No."

There was a black potbelly stove in one corner of the office and a private entered and replenished it with wood. The stove burned hot and fierce, yet the room was cold.

"Prescott, I must say I was more than a little surprised when I heard that the president was giving you permission to come here."

"How so, sir?"

"When I was told I was going to command this unit in Vladivostok, my orders were clear," the general said. "We were not to interfere in the conflict between the Reds and the Whites. I have adhered to that policy to the letter. As a result, the Reds think I am aiding the Whites, and the Whites think I am aiding the Reds. As long as they both feel that way, I suppose I am doing my job."

"I would think so, sir."

"Your presence, though, presents something of a problem. You're an officer in the United States Army—and a mighty fine one, I might add."

"Thank you, sir."

"I really wanted to get into some of that action in France. But President Wilson and Secretary Baker had other plans for me. And we do what we're told. Anyway, your presence can put our policy at risk."

"Yes, sir, the president told me as much."

"General, may I speak frankly?" Natasha asked.

"Certainly."

"Natasha, let us not be too—" Prescott said.

"He said I can be frank and I intend to be. Why should we be so concerned about what the Reds think of us? The Bolsheviks took our homes. They forced us to move into exile. It appears to me we should be doing everything in our power to help the Whites gain control."

Prescott stared at her. Her face was red and her hands trembled.

"Miss Kamarov, I commend your passion," Graves said. "But passion in the situation in which we are involved is a dangerous thing. One of my main responsibilities is to keep the TransSiberian Railway running. As long as I'm charged with that responsibility, I'm going to make sure everyone can use it—no matter the political persuasion."

"The Bolsheviks should not be permitted to use it," she said.

"You seem to think all your countrymen oppose the Bolsheviks."

"True Russian countrymen do oppose them."

"That is simply not the case. I'm here to help safeguard the territorial integrity of your country. That's supposedly why the British and French are here too. I wish I could say the same about the Japanese, but I can't. The Japanese would like to get their hands on eastern Russia. You are aware of that, aren't you? If not, you should be. As long as we're here, along with the British and French, the Japanese will not try anything."

"I'm not concerned about the Japanese," she said. "You should stop the Reds from using the railway."

"I'm sorry, but I cannot do that."

"Will I be able to meet with Kolchak soon?"

"There is time. Tonight I would like you to meet some other people."

"I do not understand," Natasha said. "Who are we to meet?"

"Some of your countrymen. They're good Russians— good people, period. I've come to learn a lot about your people, Miss Kamarov. I've come to love them—especially these people. Will you agree to visit them?"

"I do not see the point but I will."

Graves stood and put on his dark brown topcoat. He and Prescott left their cigars in the green ashtray on the desk.

"I still wish I could have been there beside you when you manned that Hotchkiss."

"It's a good thing, sir, you weren't. The man beside me was dead."

Graves led Prescott and Natasha out of the office, down the stairs, and out of the building. Even though the office was cold, the compound was much colder. Sentries snapped to attention and the general encouraged them to remain at ease. The wind blew the snow from the rooftops and

Prescott wondered why anyone would want to live in this land.

They walked down the street and said nothing. Natasha was impatient. There was work to do and the general was interfering. She did not understand him. It was preposterous to let the Reds use the railway. She wondered who these people were that she was about to meet. The general seemed in no hurry.

The street was deserted and they turned at the next intersection and came to a two-story building with a large red cross over the door. Natasha stopped.

"General, what building is this?"

"It's a hospital. It's run by the Red Cross."

"Why are we going to a hospital? Is Kolchak here?"

"I suppose in a way he is."

"What? Is he hurt? What are you saying?"

"I'm saying, Miss Kamarov, that you need to come inside."

The general pushed open the door and they walked inside. They removed their wet coats and shook them and hung them on the rack near the door. They passed through tall double doors and entered a large room which had two rows of beds, one on either side. Naked light bulbs dangled from the high ceiling. The whiteness of the sheets contrasted sharply with the dim light. Small windows ran along the tops of the walls. Through the windows there was only the blackness of the night sky. White-clad nurses moved silently from bed to bed. A man in a black suit stood at the far end of the room and stared.

The general led Prescott and Natasha between the two rows of beds. They stared at the faces of the people covered by the white sheets. They were young and old, men and women. Some of the faces were badly bruised or misshapen. Bandages covered some. There was the stench of blood that Prescott had smelled before and suddenly he was thinking of the makeshift hospitals in France and the moans of the dying. Once again he heard the moans. Some of the bodies struggled beneath the sheets against something that was trying to possess them. The nurses moved quickly and spoke barely above a whisper. Occasionally they stopped beside a bed and tried to restrain one of the bodies in its fight against the possessor. Prescott looked at Natasha. She was pale and walked limply.

They stopped at the foot of one of the beds. A boy, perhaps six or seven, with bandaged head and an arm in a cast, stared at them. A nurse stood stolidly beside him and stared without smiling at the visitors. Prescott smiled at the boy. The swollen hand beneath the cast rose. The man in the black suit adjusted the wire-rimmed spectacles on his nose and approached. The general nodded in greeting.

"This is Dr. Melakin," Graves said. "He is in charge of the ward this evening. Doctor, I want you to meet Captain Prescott Freeman and Miss Natasha Kamarov."

"Good evening, Doctor," Prescott said.

"Good evening."

The doctor's English was uncertain, strained. He eyed them coldly. He was an old, thin man whose goatee hung like ice from his chin. His gray eyes were faded and his hands trembled.

"Where are these people from?" Natasha asked.

"One of the small villages not far from here," the doctor said. "One of the villages that will never appear on a map. One of the villages that has no significance in world politics. These people were brought to the hospital yesterday. They're farmers, poor peasants, doing no one any harm."

"It matters not to the Bolsheviks who their victims are," Natasha said and she turned and surveyed the rows of beds. "Their aim is to spread fear until their authority is accepted without question."

The doctor stared at her and coughed. His hands trembled even more and his face reddened. Graves looked away.

"The Bolsheviks? You think the Bolsheviks did this?" the doctor asked. "The Bolsheviks had nothing to do with this. Kolchak's men did this."

Natasha turned quickly back to the doctor.

"Kolchak? Are you certain?"

"Yes, my dear, I am certain. At dawn yesterday Kolchak's men rode into the village and shot and beat the men, women, and children. The ones who survived lie before you."

"But—but—why?"

"The people of the village did not swear allegiance to anyone. They wanted simply to be left alone. Apparently Admiral Kolchak thinks if you do not swear allegiance to him, you are loyal to the Reds. These people know nothing of politics. For their ignorance they have paid a terrible price."

"Water," a voice behind a bandage called in Russian. "Water, please."

Soon a nurse approached with a glass.

"No, please," Natasha said, "let me."

The nurse hesitated. She stared at Natasha and slowly extended her hand. Natasha took the glass from the nurse and approached the bed. The man's face was covered with bandages except for the lips. She gently lifted his head and placed the glass next to his lips.

"God bless you," he said.

She lowered his head and touched the hand lying outside the sheet. She handed the glass to the nurse and returned to Prescott.

"I am ready to go," she said.

They walked outside and Natasha stopped and gazed at the dark, lifeless windows on the other side of the street. Her body shook. She did not want to look at the general.

"Would you like to return to the compound?"

"No," she said.

"I hope you have a clearer picture—"

"Yes, thank you, General."

Graves and Prescott shook hands and the general left them.

"Natasha, do you want to go back to the hotel?" Prescott asked.

"I just want to walk."

They walked along the sidewalks and the wind bit at them. Their noses reddened and Prescott wrapped his arm around her. Suddenly she stopped and leaned against one of the wooden columns that supported the overhang and she wept. He pulled her close to him. Then she backed away and wiped the tears with her gloved hand.

"Prescott, I am sorry. I am so sorry."

"What happened to those people was not your fault."

"What I have done to you is my fault. I've brought you here to something that is not at all what I expected."

"We live in a world that has been turned upside down," he said. "It's hard to know what to expect anymore."

"I have used you, Prescott. I have used you and I should not have. In Paris soldiers talked about you, about your fearlessness in the face of death. I wanted to meet such a man. I knew such a man could help me and my countrymen. And so I wanted to meet you and you were everything I expected. I wanted to use you but then I fell in love with you and still I used you."

"You did not use me. Natasha, I am a big boy. No one forced me to come here. It was my decision."

"But I feel I have used you poorly—and for what? I thought Kolchak was a patriot. A patriot would not do what he has done."

"We should return to Paris," he said. "There is nothing here for you, Natasha. You have to recognize that. Let's go back to Paris. We will be married—in one of the great cathedrals."

"After all this, after all that I have put you through, you want to marry me?"

"I assure you I have been through much worse. We will marry in Paris and your father and mother will come to like me."

"Will the president be your best man?"

"I am not sure his schedule will permit that. If Harry is still in Paris when we return, he will be my best man. And then I will take you back to Georgia as my wife."

"And I will see you play baseball?"

"Yes, you will see me play baseball. So—what is your answer, Princess Natasha? Will you be my wife?"

"Yes, Captain Freeman, I will be your wife."

Her face darkened.

"I made a promise to those who came with us," she said. "I said I would get them to Kolchak. I cannot simply leave them here. I am responsible for them."

"Just tell them what you saw tonight."

"I will. But if they still insist on joining forces with Kolchak, I have to help them. I gave them my word. I am their leader. You must understand. After I deliver them, I will return to Paris with you and we will be married and Harry Truman will be your best man."

"I will talk to the general tomorrow. I will explain your feelings. I am sure he will not like it, but perhaps he will provide an escort for us."

He lowered his head and kissed her. Her eyes were still moist.

"I need to get you out of the cold," he said.

They stepped onto the silent street and walked toward the hotel. He glanced at the buildings. The windows were like unfathomable eyes spying upon them.

"I look forward to this game of baseball," she said.

Walton Young

CHAPTER FIFTEEN

Prescott and Natasha met with her countrymen in the coldness of the hotel dining room the next morning. No one except the old woman who ran the place was around. Prescott once again did not understand what was being said, but he understood. The tables were close together and little warmth came from the stove in the corner. Natasha spoke quietly, slowly. The eyes of the others flashed with anger. Their voices came at once.

"They think General Graves is trying to deceive us," she said.

"Tell them it is not in the general's interest to deceive anyone," Prescott said.

"It will do no good. I have told them we should all return to Paris, but they refuse. I must lead them to Kolchak."

"Very well. I will speak to the general."

The men stared at Prescott. They did not trust General Graves. They did not trust Prescott. And now they did not trust Natasha. Any war was bad, Prescott thought. But civil war was the worst. The stories he heard while growing up came in and out of his mind. Brother fighting brother. . . . Hatred that would not die.

Prescott left Natasha and the others at the hotel and went to the compound. Graves was in his office.

"Natasha and I have decided to return to Paris," Prescott said.

"That is a wise decision."

"But she promised the men who came with us to take them to Kolchak. She feels she must stay true to her promise."

The general leaned back in his chair and stared for a moment at the ceiling.

"You need to steer clear of Kolchak. He's a murderer. He calls himself a liberator. But he's nothing but a murderer."

"Natasha will not go back on her word. The others insist on moving forward with their plans."

Graves shook his head.

"Prescott, you've gotten involved in a bad situation. It's none of my business, but you love this woman, don't you?"

"Yes, sir."

"I'm afraid that in the world in which we now live love can get you killed. I'll have Major Jones put together a small contingent of troops. We'll provide some wagons and supplies. We know the location of Kolchak's headquarters. Jones will escort you there."

"Thank you, sir. Once the men meet up with Kolchak, Natasha and I will go back to Paris. We're going to get married."

"I wish both of you the best. I just hope you live long enough to get married. Good luck, Captain."

❧

PRESCOTT AND NATASHA AND THEIR entourage gathered before dawn the next day at the stables inside the compound. Guards escorted them and watched them carefully. The snow came during the night and now fell heavily. Their footprints quickly became lost. Lanterns hung from rafters and the breath from the horses shone bright. Jones, accompanied by six soldiers with carbines slung over their shoulders, walked into the barn. Natasha wore a long, black leather coat with mink around the collar. Jones stared.

"Looks as if you folks are ready to travel," Jones said.

"How long will it take us?" Prescott asked.

"Oh, probably a day and a half. Of course the snow's bad. It may take longer. Also, we may get delayed."

"Why?"

"We've received threats lately. The Reds and Whites are never happy with us. We just can't seem to please either one of them. You have to understand—if they fire at us, we'll fire back. You know how it is. Fighting takes time. It could delay us. Where have you put your weapons?"

"They're in one of the wagons," Prescott said.

"Good. Your friends can ride in the wagons. Natasha, do you prefer riding in the wagon or on horseback?"

"Horseback."

Prescott picked out a gray mare and helped Natasha mount the saddle. The horses snorted and pawed the straw-strewn ground. Prescott took in the smell of leather and hay, something he had not done since he left home. He patted the rear flank of the horse and then went to find one of his own. Away from the others he stopped and felt the pistol in the holster. Jones stood beside him.

"Look, Prescott, something I want to tell you. That business about the Reds and Whites taking shots at us. I wasn't joking."

"I understand."

"We'll probably have no trouble. But it is a war."

"I know."

"And civil war is the worst kind—especially if you find yourself in the middle of it."

They rode out of the barn into the snowy darkness and proceeded along a street at the rear of the town. Wood smoke hung in the air. The wagon wheels creaked and there was no talking. An old man delivering milk stopped and watched.

"I was hoping we'd get out of town without being seen," Jones said.

Prescott rode beside Natasha. She did not smile. She did not talk. Grimness hung on her face as the Russian winter held onto the countryside. From the rear the buildings looked like shacks that had sprung up alongside railroad tracks. The sharp piercing whistle of a locomotive cried and Natasha shuddered. Prescott reached over and touched her hand.

Prescott saw no road. There was only snow. They left the outskirts of the town and entered a wasteland of white. There were no houses, no barns, no fences, no people, just the endless ocean of snow. The clouds hung gray and low but the wind died. The horses struggled but still they moved on.

"Not like the terrain in Georgia," Jones said.

"It'd be nice to see a pine tree."

"We'll see trees this afternoon. I know a good spot for a bivouac."

Again the locomotive screamed but it was far away now. Prescott tried to imagine travelers on the train. He wondered where they would be going in this wilderness of white. He looked over his shoulder. There was no sign of smoke. He glanced at the two wagons. Natasha's compatriots sat huddled in two black masses, their heads bowed upon their chests. They did not speak. They did not look at the countryside.

"Not a talkative group, are they?" Jones asked.

"They don't trust Americans."

"I understand. I don't trust Russians. General Graves cares more about them than I do."

"I'm concerned about Kolchak. When he sees us coming—"

"Before we left this morning, I sent a soldier who knows him to tell him we're coming."

Prescott wondered about surprise attacks. There was no place for assailants to hide unless they buried themselves in the snow. But then there would be the trees.

The morning passed slowly. The soldiers followed the wagons and talked and occasionally laughed. Some spat dark tobacco juice upon the whiteness. For the most part they were young, little more than boys. They probably came from farms, eager to leave the hard work of the land for the adventure of the military. Their adventure now lay in Siberia, certainly not what they had expected. On the horizon a speck appeared. Prescott studied it—a farmhouse, the first one he had seen since leaving Vladivostok. A thin ribbon of smoke hovered from the chimney and quickly became lost in the grayness of the day. He considered the kind of people that would live in a wilderness like this and he remembered the people in the hospital. He could see the swollen and bruised faces. He could hear the low moans.

He could smell the odor of blood. He would never be able to forget those things. He had found them in France and he had found them again in Siberia. The setting could change but the sight, sound, and smell of battle always remained the same.

"How far have we come?" Natasha asked in the early afternoon.

"Many miles," Prescott said. "I cannot say for sure."

"Tell me about Georgia."

He turned and she smiled. It was the first smile he had seen since they left early in the morning.

"Right now it is late spring. The fields have been plowed. They are red in the sun. They will grow the finest cotton and corn you have ever seen. There is rain—no snow."

"I cannot wait to see your home. Do you think your family will like me?"

"They will love you."

"After we go to your home, how soon will you play baseball?"

"In the summer. I will hit a home run for you."

"What is a home run?"

"You will know when you see it."

The sky grew dark. Prescott saw something else on the horizon. Trees rose like specters in the snow.

"What did I tell you?" Jones asked. "That's where we'll bivouac tonight."

The forest was like an island in the snow. The soldiers pitched pup tents and gathered wood for a fire. Prescott helped Natasha to the ground and they stretched and felt the soreness in their bodies. The Russians climbed wearily out of the wagons and stood awkwardly near the stack of wood that would soon crackle into a flame. The spruces and firs hovered above them and sheltered them from the wind that was rising in the west. Daylight was fading.

"I need a moment of privacy," Natasha said.

"Go behind a tree," Prescott said.

She smirked and was gone. Prescott looked around. Jones had chosen a good spot for the camp.

"How deep is the forest?" Prescott asked.

"Not as deep as it appears," Jones answered.

"And on the other side?"

"More of what we've just crossed. We'll pass some villages, or at least what's left of them."

A sergeant organized pots and pans and tin cans on the ground close to the fire and prepared the meal. The aroma of coffee drifted among the trees. Natasha returned and wrapped her arm inside Prescott's. They stood by the fire and the sergeant opened the cans.

"Sir, my name's O'Malley," the sergeant said. "I hope you and the missus like beans and soup. They make perfect eating on a night like tonight."

The lonely howl of a wolf pierced the air and one of the soldiers retrieved a carbine from his horse. Prescott patted Natasha's hand.

"He is just welcoming us," Prescott said.

"That's right, sir," the sergeant said, and he poured coffee into a tin cup and offered it to Natasha. He poured another and handed it to Prescott. "Them wolves sure make a lot of noise. But they ain't going to bother us."

The sergeant scooped beans and soup into bowls and handed them to the Russians and then to the soldiers. In the bitter cold of twilight the food tasted delicious to Prescott. Even Natasha seemed to enjoy it. The major sat under a tree near them and between bites talked about the mountains of Tennessee. He said he had a difficult time getting used to the endless flatlands covered with snow.

"Give me a tree and I feel right at home," Jones said. "Well, I'd better post sentries for the night. We'll leave before daybreak."

Darkness fell heavily on the forest and the flames from the fire shot skyward and flung sparks into the lower reaches of the trees. Some of the soldiers sat close to the fire and played cards. One soldier sat against the back wheel of a wagon and played a harmonica. Prescott did not know the song. It was slow and mournful. He wished he would stop. The Russians huddled together and seldom spoke. Occasionally they looked at Natasha. Their eyes were black and bitter.

CHAPTER SIXTEEN

During the night Prescott slept little. Natasha lay in a pup tent. Near the flap of her tent one of the soldiers kept a fire going. Occasionally the wolf cried and then there was silence. Prescott gave up on sleep and stood and walked toward the horses. Jones was also up.

"It's hard to sleep with that wolf making so much noise," Jones said.

"Wolf or no wolf, I don't think I would be able to sleep."

"Prescott, one of the sentries heard something a little while ago.

"What did he hear?"

"He thought he heard some rustling among bushes at the edge of the forest. He said he couldn't be sure."

"Is he experienced?"

"Yes. Do you want to turn back?"

Prescott shook his head.

"I'll have two of my men ride ahead just as a precaution," Jones said. "There's probably nothing to worry about."

O'Malley already had bacon sizzling over the fire, and Prescott took a cup of coffee to Natasha and waked her gently. The other Russians were stirring. Prescott looked at them and wondered.

Several soldiers brought their shovels and tossed snow onto the campfire. The party mounted the horses and wagons and moved slowly north through the forest. Prescott listened. There was complete silence. There were no birds. The wolves were gone. There were just the trees and the party on its way to meet with Kolchak. He and Natasha rode close to the first wagon. Up ahead, almost out of view, were the two soldiers riding the point.

And the forest ended. Ahead was another endless plain of snow. They spent the morning crossing it. The wind and the snow tore at them as if to drive them back. By late morning they came to a small village, a smoldering ruin. Near what appeared to be the entrance to a hut a tiny doll lay smudged in the snow. There were no signs of life. The party passed and no one spoke. Natasha stared at the ruins and bowed her head. Her lips moved silently.

Some two miles north of the village another forest loomed. More spruces and firs rose against the horizon. Prescott reined his horse.

"What is it?" Natasha asked.

He did not answer. The two soldiers riding the point were almost to the edge of the trees. The snow was deep and the horses struggled. White breath rushed from their nostrils. Jones rode up to Prescott.

"Everything appears to be all right," Jones said.

The rest of the party moved slowly. The snow fell and the wind blew the flakes into their faces. Prescott removed his right glove.

"Love, what are you doing?" she asked. "Your hand will get frostbite."

He reached for the holster and withdrew his pistol.

"Love, you do not need that."

Prescott watched the two soldiers. They stopped and turned and waved their hands.

"Yeah, I was right," Jones said. "Everything is all right."

The party was drawing closer to the two soldiers and the wind was now stronger. It stung their faces but they kept moving. The horses stumbled in the drifts.

There was an explosion and a screaming cannon shell burst the snow in front of the wagons. Suddenly the woods on the other side were aflame with rifle fire. The soldiers riding point were gunned down. Jones was hollering orders to his soldiers. Prescott reached out for Natasha but her horse broke free. Another cannon shell exploded in the heart of the first wagon, where the rifles and ammunition were kept. Another explosion and fire sent men screaming into the volley of gunfire. Prescott's horse fell and he rolled onto the snow. Jones looked down from his saddle and stretched forth his hand. A rifle bullet ripped through his throat and he fell. He lay writhing on the snow and grabbed at his throat and gasped for breath.

"Prescott! Prescott!"

Natasha's horse was down and she was running toward him. Machine gun bullets splintered the snow and flung it against his body. He ran toward her and fired his pistol toward the woods. A bullet ripped the skin on his cheek and he stumbled and regained his balance. The smell of gun smoke was heavy in the air. The other soldiers sought shelter behind the remaining wagon and fired their carbines furiously.

"Prescott! Prescott!"

It was almost impossible to run in the deep snow and the bullets whizzed past them.

"Hurry, Captain!" one of the soldiers yelled.

The machine guns rattled and then there was another explosion. The cannon shell bit heavily into his leg and he flew through the air. He turned over on his stomach and tried to find Natasha.

"Natasha! Natasha!"

The nausea and faintness gripped his body and his vision blurred. He strained to see through the smoke. And then he saw her. She had almost reached him. She was lying on her side. There was blood. Bright red blood stained the whiteness of the snow. And then the world became black.

PRESCOTT OPENED HIS EYES. A naked light bulb dangled on a wire above him. At least he thought it was a wire. He could not tell. His head ached. He did not know where he was but he knew he was inside a building. He knew because he felt the cot beneath him and there was warmth, more warmth than he had felt in a long time. There were people standing around him but he could not see their faces.

"Natasha," he said and he started to get up.

Hands pressed against his shoulders but he could not see the bodies attached to the hands.

"Let me go!" he said. "I must find Natasha!"

"Please, sir, please lie back down."

The voice, a woman's, was soft and soothing. It was American.

"Where am I?"

"You are in the Red Cross hospital in Vladivostok. General Graves has been summoned."

He closed his eyes and smelled the disinfectant. He opened his eyes again and began to see more clearly. Two nurses stood on either side of the cot and the old doctor stood at the foot. He remembered his leg and he reached his hand down to feel.

"It is still there, Captain," the doctor said. "You were lucky. We did not have to amputate."

Lucky, he said to himself, and he thought about Natasha. He saw her body lying in the snow. He saw the blood. He saw Jones's face with the bloody hole in the throat. The naked light bulb blinked.

"How long have I been unconscious?" he asked.

"Three days," the doctor said. "For a while we were not certain you would survive. You lost much blood."

"And the others?"

"General Graves is coming to talk to you. He will tell you what you need to know."

Prescott closed his eyes. The pain in his leg was scalding and he winced.

"Do you want morphine?" the doctor asked.

"No. I must have a clear head to talk to the general."

Other patients were talking in Russian. He imagined they were talking about him. They were probably wondering what an American soldier was doing here, wounded. Suddenly he thought about the Argonne. He had escaped without a wound. So many had fallen. And now, here in Siberia, he was cut down.

"Good afternoon, General," the doctor said.

Prescott opened his eyes. The focus was returning. General Graves removed his hat and nodded at Prescott. He did not smile.

"I want to know about Natasha," Prescott said.

One of the nurses brought a chair and the general sat near the head of the bed. The doctor and the nurses walked away.

"After you were wounded, some of our troops managed to drag you to the wagon. A British patrol was in the area. They heard the gunfire and they came as quickly as possible. For many, it was too late."

"Natasha? I want to know about Natasha."

The general ran his hand over his chin and looked at the floor.

"I'm sorry, Prescott. She didn't make it. One of the troops reported she was killed. They tried to save as many as they could, but there was nothing they could do. I'm sorry, Prescott. I truly am."

Prescott gripped the sides of the cot tightly and he closed his eyes.

"They left her?"

"Prescott, they had no choice. You knew what the gunfire was like. It was intense, according to the reports I've seen. We lost several of our men. We lost Major Jones."

"Yes. He was reaching out his hand, trying to help me when he was hit. He was a good man."

"One of the best I've had the privilege of serving with. I'm going to write that in the letter to his parents."

"Who were the ones who attacked?"

"I can't say for sure. Indications are they were Bolsheviks. We received word that they're claiming responsibility. They think I'm doing too much for the Whites."

"I have to get out of here and find her body."

"No."

"What do you mean?"

"You're going to have to recuperate. It's going to take some time. Also, the president has been informed of the attack. You're being ordered to return to Paris."

"Back to Paris? I can't leave—not now. I can't return without her. I owe it to her parents. How can I look them in the eye and tell them I left her in the middle of a wilderness? How can I do that, General?"

"You have no choice, son. Those are your orders and they come from the highest levels of our government. Look—there is nothing you can do here now. There is nothing you can do to help Natasha. I have many contacts. I stand a much better chance of finding her body. You've got to concentrate on getting better. The doctor tells me you won't be able to travel for several weeks. As bad as things are, they could be worse. You could be dead also like the others. That's a nasty wound in your leg. At least you got to keep it."

"The doctor has already told me how lucky I am."

"And you are."

The general stood and turned to go.

"General."

Graves stopped.

"Yes, son."

"Thanks. I really do appreciate what you've done."

"I wish I could have done a lot more, Prescott. A lot more."

Walton Young

CHAPTER SEVENTEEN

In the darkness of the bedroom Prescott sat in a split-bottom chair next to the window and stared. The snow lay even, peaceful. He knew that whenever he saw the snow, he would not see the white but the red, the blood. Natasha should be with him now. He should have never taken her back to Russia. She was headstrong, but he should have prevailed. He bowed his head and called her name in the silence of the room. He closed his eyes and saw. Her body lay crumpled on the snow. The bullets whizzed past his head. He would always hear them. And then he thought of his grandfather, Jeffrey. All the battles, all the gunfire. . . . He wondered whether Jeffrey always heard the bullets zipping past his head. He wanted to talk to him. There was no one else. He wanted to talk to his grandfather because he would know what war was like.

Jeffrey knew war. He knew vengeance. Charley Kell killed Jeffrey's brother. Prescott had heard the story. Jeffrey swore vengeance and followed Kell across Georgia, across the South, into the West. He followed him and he caught up with him and he killed him. And the violence continued. Prescott breathed deeply. He knew what it was to kill. And then the people close to him died.

The knock at first was distant. It grew louder, desperate. Prescott stood and listened. There was a flurry of footsteps. He quickly left his room and hurried downstairs. The door to the main hall was open. The family was huddled around a visitor, but Thaddeus stood at the rear of the others. He simply glanced at his oldest son. Prescott moved closer.

"Galen!" William said. "Where on earth have you been?"

Galen stumbled forward. He was not alone. Verlon supported him and helped him into the hall.

"Galen!" Grandma Freeman called. "Son, are you hurt?"

"He's just mighty cold, Ma," Verlon said. "We need to get him to a fire."

"Help him into the parlor," she said. "Mandy, run upstairs and get him some clothes. William, go to the blanket chest in my room. Bring a couple of quilts. And hurry up."

Sam pulled up a wing chair close to the fire. Henry tossed a couple of logs onto the andirons. It was not long until Mandy returned with an armful of clothes. William was close behind with two patchwork quilts in his arms.

"All right, I want the rest of you to leave," Grandma Freeman said. "Verlon, you stay and help me get him into these warm clothes."

She closed the door behind them. Thaddeus stood in the hall. His face was pale and Prescott went up to him.

"Pa, do you want a chair?"

"No, son, I'm all right."

"Why don't you wait in the study?"

Thaddeus shook his head and stared at the closed door. On the other side were his mother, one of his sons, and a brother who had not set foot inside the house in years. Thaddeus kept telling himself he should be in the parlor. It was his house, but he could not move. There were many things he understood. This was not one of them. He did not understand why Galen would be coming in at such a late hour on a night like tonight, and he could not understand why his brother would be here. He should go in the parlor. Still, he did not move.

Henry put his arm around Mandy's shoulder.

"Can I get you anything?" Henry asked.

"No. I just want to know what's going on. Galen looked terrible. Pres, did you notice? Galen looked terrible."

Prescott reached into his shirt pocket for a cigarette and struck a match and inhaled deeply.

"Why do you think Galen was with Uncle Verlon?" Sam asked.

"No need to ask questions," Mandy said. "We'll know soon enough. Pa, maybe you should be in there. They may need you."

Thaddeus looked at his daughter as if she were a stranger. Slowly he started across the hall but then stopped.

"William, you and Sam see to your Uncle Verlon's mules," Thaddeus said.

He went to the door. On the other side there was silence. He reached out and turned the doorknob and went into the parlor.

Inside the parlor wet clothes were stacked on the heart pine floor and his mother and brother were helping Galen into a red flannel shirt. Galen was shivering. Grandma Freeman tucked one of the quilts around him.

"Brother, you got any bourbon around here?" Verlon asked. "It'll get Galen's blood pumping faster. It won't do mine no harm neither."

Thaddeus walked to the mahogany corner cabinet and poured bourbon from the decanter into three glasses.

"Ma?"

"No thanks. I'm going to brew some tea. I think hot tea will do a better job of warming him up."

Thaddeus handed a glass to his brother and to his son.

"Galen, where have you been?" Thaddeus asked.

Galen sipped the bourbon and coughed. Grandma Freeman swept up the wet clothes in her arms and left. The others stayed in the hall.

"Just watching and waiting," Galen said and his eyes never left the flames. "Waiting and watching—until the end came. And then I went to Uncle Verlon's."

"I don't understand, son," Thaddeus said. "You still haven't said where you were."

This time Galen lifted the glass and downed the drink in one gulp and set the glass on a table. The fire hissed and sparks defied the downdraft and flew up the chimney.

"I sat on the hill overlooking Ledbetter's place."

Verlon looked at his brother. In the glow of the firelight fear shone in Thaddeus's eyes.

"Ledbetter's?"

"That's right, Pa. I sat there all evening. It's a beautiful sight—watching the snow come down in the twilight. Each flake has its own little share of gray daylight and so you have a million little pale lights sprinkling down from heaven and lighting the ground. I had never noticed it before but, then, I had never sat on a hill like that."

"Why did you go there?" Thaddeus asked.

"I wanted to be close to her. I knew she was going to die. I heard the screech owl. I knew it was crying for her."

"Nobody was going to die."

"You're wrong, Pa. Emma is dead. I sat on that hill and watched and waited. The doc came. The preacher and his family came. I should have gone inside. That was where I should have been. But I sat on top of the hill and watched and waited. I knew Emma was dead. I killed her, Pa."

"No, nonsense, Galen."

"I killed her. Her blood is on me. Blood has always been the most important thing in this family. That's what I've always heard. But now somebody else's blood is mingled with my blood. Your investment didn't pay off too well, did it?"

"What investment?"

"The money you paid old man Ledbetter. Just think—if you'd waited a little longer, you wouldn't have had to pay him a cent. But he got your money. I call that a bad investment. What do you call that, Uncle Verlon?

"Oh, I don't know, son," Verlon said. "It sounds like one of the crazy roads life leads us down. You want another drink? I think it might help you feel better."

"I ain't used to the liquor," Galen said. "I'm feeling kind of sleepy. I just want to sleep a long time. And I want to forget. I want to forget everything. I want to forget that tonight I was responsible for someone's death. I loved her, Pa. And I killed her, just as surely as if I had picked up a gun and shot her."

Galen closed his eyes but the tears were already upon his cheeks. Verlon went to the corner cabinet and poured another drink.

"Well, I think he is going to get his wish," Verlon said. "I'm sure he will sleep for a while. The boy is spent, completely spent."

Thaddeus stared at his son. Heat from the fire spread throughout the room and Galen soon was asleep. He would not need the tea Grandma Freeman was brewing. Thaddeus walked close to his son and reached his hand out and softly touched his shoulder.

"This is not a good night to wander the countryside," Verlon said.

"Thank you for bringing him home."

The two men looked at each other for a moment and looked away.

"You don't have to thank me," Verlon said. "When he showed up at my place, I knew you folks would be worried sick about him, so I loaded him up into the wagon and drove him over."

Verlon looked around the room. The Christmas tree stood in the opposite corner. Magnolia leaves and pine cones lay on the mantel. He remembered. As boys he and Thaddeus sat in this room on cold winter nights. Their father told stories about hunting and fishing, but Thaddeus never seemed interested. His mind would wander and then he would leave the room. Verlon would continue to sit on the couch next to Jeffrey and listen to the tales. He took in every word. He remembered the stories about the panther that came down from the mountains and cried mournfully in the darkness. Jeffrey explained that the panther had probably lost its mate and was crying for it. But all the farmers were wary. They got their shotguns and rifles and went into the woods to look for it. They found paw prints along the edge of the Etowah but they never saw the panther. Some of the old-timers still said they heard it in the dead of night.

Grandma Freeman returned with the tea on a tray and looked down at Galen. She set the tray on the table in front of the sofa. She placed the back of her hand against Galen's forehead.

"He's warm, but it's from the fire," she said. "I don't think he has a fever. We can be thankful for that."

She sat in the chair near the Christmas tree.

"Well, it's been a long time since the three of us occupied this room," she said. "Verlon, as always we missed you at Christmas dinner."

"You know me, Ma," Verlon said, "I ain't much for big family gatherings. I reckon I best be on my way."

"No, wait—" Thaddeus said. "It's late. The weather's miserable. We've taken care of your mules. You should stay here tonight."

Verlon bit his lower lip.

"You're sure I won't be any trouble?"

"No. You won't be any trouble. We'd be—pleased—to have you."

Verlon struggled but he managed to smile.

"Ma, why don't you go to bed?" Verlon asked. "Thaddeus and I will sit up with the boy. You need to rest."

"No, I need to be right here," she said. "If I get tired, I'll stretch out on the sofa."

"Thaddeus, there's something we need to talk about."

Thaddeus grew uncomfortable. After all the years, it was too late to talk.

"I'm talking about Ledbetter," Verlon said.

"What about him?"

"I don't know if Emma is dead. Galen said she is. But I'm not sure Galen is quite in his right mind. But if what he says is true, if that girl is dead, Ledbetter ain't going to blame Galen as much as he's going to blame you. He'll try to kill you."

Thaddeus realized he had not tasted the bourbon. He lifted the glass to his lips and drank. The bourbon went down hot and smooth. He smiled.

"Let him try," Thaddeus said.

"I've heard men talk," Verlon said. "They tell how Ledbetter has bragged about the day that's coming, the day he's going to kill you."

"We shouldn't talk about this in front of Ma."

"Yes, you should," Grandma Freeman said. "Verlon is right. Ledbetter hates you. If Emma is dead, there's no telling what he'll try. Maybe we should call the sheriff. Maybe he could post a deputy—"

"There's no need to call the sheriff. I've handled Ledbetter all these years. I can handle him now. Like I said, if he wants to try something, let him try. Ma, don't look so worried. When I go into town, I carry a pistol. I still know how to fire the thing."

"A pistol won't do much good against Ledbetter's shotgun," Verlon said.

"If a Freeman and a Ledbetter are in a fight, a Freeman is always going to win. It's just the way the world is. A Freeman is going to win."

Verlon sat on the sofa and looked at Galen. The boy was sleeping soundly but the breathing made hardly a sound. He thought about the look in Galen's eyes earlier. It was as if he had checked out of life for a while and left no forwarding address. Verlon did not like that look. He had never seen it before and he never wanted to see it again. He glanced up at his brother. Maybe Ledbetter had already won and Thaddeus just did not know it. Maybe Ledbetter held all the cards and Thaddeus just did not see.

"Ledbetter is a mean old cuss," Verlon said.

"He's a varmint," Thaddeus said. "The Ledbetter has not been born that I cannot handle. Trust me. I know what I'm doing."

CHAPTER EIGHTEEN

"I've got to do something," Mandy said. "This standing around is killing me. I'm going to the kitchen and cook breakfast."

"It's a little early for breakfast," William said.

"Then don't eat."

"Henry, your folks know where you are, don't they?" Prescott asked.

"Yeah."

"You take one of the rooms upstairs if you're tired."

"I don't think I could sleep right now. I think I'll help Mandy in the kitchen."

Prescott, along with William and Sam, went into the dining room and sat at the long table. He had never seen his brothers so quiet. They simply sat and stared at the fireplace that had grown cold.

"I think I'll get a fire going," Prescott said. "It's cold in here."

The pine kindling caught quickly and he tossed a couple of rough hickory logs onto the bright red flames. Mandy opened the icebox to get thick strips of bacon, but Rap leaped up and ran out of the kitchen. She watched him and shook her head. The dog hurried to Prescott and leaned against his legs.

"Why aren't you in the kitchen, boy? That's where the food is. Where are your buddies? Mandy, are the other dogs in there?"

"No. They ran upstairs. Pretty strange."

Prescott ran his hand across the bird dog's back. Rap was trembling.

"What's wrong, boy?"

The scream came from just outside the window. Rap crouched and whimpered. William and Sam jumped to their feet and Mandy ran into the dining room. The scream was a loud, sudden woman's shriek. Mandy thrust the bacon back into the icebox and slammed the door.

"Prescott, what is it?" Mandy asked. "Is there a woman out there?"

"No. There's no woman out there. It's a panther."

"I'm getting a shotgun," Sam said.

"You're doing no such thing," Mandy said.

"Maybe we should all go out there," Henry said.

The scream was louder the second time and Rap leaped to his feet and ran out of the dining room and joined the other dogs at the top of the back stairs. Mandy grabbed hold of Prescott's arm.

"Pres, what should we do?"

"Nothing. It'll move on in a minute. Henry, you still want to go out there?"

"No. On second thought, I think I'll stay put."

"That's a wise decision," Prescott said. "He's just lonely. He's looking for a little companionship. When he doesn't find it here, he'll go to another farm."

"How do you know it's going to move on?" William asked.

"I just know."

"Why would a panther come here?" Mandy asked.

"It's come down out of the mountains," Prescott said. "He's probably lost his mate. He's come here looking for her. That's just what panthers do. Henry, you look pretty white. Maybe you'd better sit down."

Prescott said no more. He remembered the stories Verlon told him. Panthers smelled death and tonight death hung over Kingston.

"Hey, what's wrong with you folks?"

Mandy jumped and turned quickly as if expecting to confront the black image of a panther that was ready to spring. Verlon grinned.

"Mandy, it's just me. What's going on?"

"You didn't hear that?" William asked.

"Hear what? What are you talking about?"

"That scream," Sam said. "My blood is still running cold. It sounded just like a woman about to die."

The grin on Verlon's face disappeared.

"Pres, do you think it was a panther?"

"I think so. But it's gone now."

Verlon walked to the window and looked out. He saw nothing in the blackness but the pale whiteness of the snow. He breathed heavily. He did not like panthers. He did not like their scream, especially on a night like tonight.

"How is Galen?" Mandy asked.

"He's sleeping. Mandy, sugar, is there any coffee? It's going to be a long night. Ma doesn't want me to have any more bourbon, so it's time to move on to coffee."

"Sure. Come into the kitchen."

Verlon left the window and started toward the kitchen.

"None of you heard that scream?" William asked.

"No," Verlon said. "We didn't hear a thing. Maybe you just dreamed it."

"Tell that to the dogs."

"Well, bird dogs want no part of a panther," Verlon said. "That's a fact."

He followed Mandy to the kitchen, but he stopped at the door. She poured coffee into a white china cup and turned.

"Well, Verlon, here it is. Why don't you come into the kitchen?"

He glanced around the kitchen—at the black-and-white wood-burning stove with the warmer on top, at the pine work table in the middle, at the pie safe, at the old dry sink. All this was his mother's. But it was also Abigail's. This was the room that was truly hers. It was her domain. He looked at the stove. He had never seen her in this kitchen, but now he saw her. He looked at the work table and saw her. A clear whiskey bottle stood upright on the table. He saw her. She rolled biscuit dough with the bottle.

"Verlon, are you all right? Come get your coffee."

His feet did not want to cross the threshold. He was an interloper. This was her terrain and now that she was gone he was about to trespass.

"Oh, all right, here."

Mandy took the cup to him and he accepted it carefully. She looked at him strangely.

"Henry is going to have funny ideas about my family."

Henry did not hear her comment. He focused on the window as if expecting to see the white fangs of the panther. At any moment he expected to hear the glass shattering. Mandy returned to the icebox. Soon the bacon was frying in an iron skillet.

She brought the bacon and eggs to the table. Verlon joined William and Sam on the bench and Prescott and Henry sat in chairs. She poured coffee and they ate slowly.

"Pres, I haven't heard you say that you're staying for sure, no ifs, ands, or buts," Mandy said. "Tell me you're staying."

Prescott sipped the steaming coffee. George Marshall waited to hear the answer also. Patton had told him he was a fool if he did not stay in but, then, that was Patton.

"Maybe Pres needs a bit more time before he makes a decision," Verlon said.

"Who would want to stay around this mess?" Sam asked. "Pres, if you want to return to the army, I wouldn't blame you. If you stay here, look at what you've got to deal with."

"Hush your mouth," Mandy said. "That kind of talk isn't necessary. Pres belongs here. This is his home, mess or no mess."

Sam stood suddenly and walked out of the dining room and went up the stairs. Mandy started to rise.

"Let him be," Verlon said. "He's still a pup. He's having to deal with an awful lot for someone as young as he is."

"Uncle Verlon, I sure wish you'd come around sometimes," William said. "It's nice to have a level head on the place. Pres has a level head, but he's an adventurer. Don't look that way, Pres. You know you are. You won't answer Mandy because you know you ain't staying. But I agree with Sam. I don't blame you for leaving, not one bit. I think I will check on Sam."

William walked out and Mandy set her knife and fork carefully on top of the scrambled eggs.

"Well, I reckon my cooking isn't all that good," she said. "It seems to run everybody off."

"Nonsense," Verlon said. "Look at Pres and me. We're putting it away. Darn good cooking, Mandy dear. Don't you be putting yourself down any, you hear?"

"Henry, you're not eating," she said.

"I can't get the sound of that panther—or whatever it was—out of my head," Henry said. "It's still screaming in my ears."

"All the more reason to eat, son," Verlon said.

"I think I will call it a night. Good night, Mandy."

Henry left and Mandy's shoulders sagged.

"I don't think Henry will want any part of this family after tonight," she said.

"There you go putting yourself down again," Verlon said. "Henry's a fine boy. He's crazy about you."

She stood and took her plate into the kitchen and scraped the eggs into the large can in the corner.

"It's good to have you here," Prescott said. "You haven't been here since—"

"Since your pa and ma got married. A long time ago. I sit here and realize just how long ago it was."

Prescott and Verlon lit cigarettes and smoked.

"I hope you do stay," Verlon said. "I know what everybody says—about how hard it is for a country boy to stay put on the farm after seeing all the bright lights. But this is where you belong. That's my two cents' worth, and my opinion is worth just that amount."

"We'll see."

"Call on that Avanelle girl. She's a beautiful lass."

"I can't think about that now."

"I take it there's been someone else."

"Yes."

"Well then, marry the someone else and settle down and raise a bunch of kids."

"She's dead."

Verlon removed the cigarette from his lips and stared at Prescott. Then he lowered his head and stared at the table.

"Pres, I'm sorry. I didn't know. Me and my big mouth. That's what comes from living alone, I guess. You just don't know when to open your mouth and when to keep it shut. I am really sorry. Does your pa know?"

"No. I haven't told him. I just haven't wanted to talk about it."

"You should talk to Thaddeus. He's your father. He can help you."

"Can he?"

Prescott thought about Galen. Thaddeus had helped him. Prescott exhaled the smoke and stared at the wide plank floor. There they were—the dark spots, some large, some small, left years ago from soldiers gray and blue who had lain in this room with a doctor working feverishly over them. In '64 those spots on the floor were bright red. Now they were simply dark, almost black. They were an indelible part of the floor. He would always remember them.

Walton Young

CHAPTER NINETEEN

For hours Avanelle could not sleep. She sat on the floor at the foot of Emma's bed. Her mother, the baby in a blanket in her lap, sat in a cane-bottom chair that had been brought into the small bedroom. She had used a medicine dropper to give milk to the baby, and now the baby slept. Elizabeth's eyes were closed and she breathed softly. Myrtle, her face almost as white as her daughter's, sat in a rocking chair and stared at Emma. Occasionally she would reach out and touch the cold hands. She would not permit the sheet to be pulled over Emma's face. There was an incredible stillness in the house and, to Avanelle, it was more than the stillness of death that had occurred. It was the stillness of death to come. She was afraid. Her back ached and she wanted to stand, but she was concerned her movements would disturb her mother. She needed rest.

In the other room the fire had died, but no one heeded the cold. McIntosh, the worn black Bible open in his lap, sat in a chair and slept. Emma's brothers lay on the floor near the silent fireplace and slept. Ledbetter stood by the door and surveyed the room. He too heard the stillness.

Redness crept up the window. Even the roosters remained quiet. Nothing ventured outside on a morning like this, but he knew he must. He knew what had to be done. The day of reckoning had arrived.

He lifted his heavy black coat and put it on and walked softly to the small table where he kept shotgun shells. He put several in his coat pocket. Then he wrapped his hands around the shotgun standing in the corner. He looked around. Everyone slept. Let them sleep, he said to himself. There was work to do and only he could do it.

The door closed and Avanelle opened her eyes. She was surprised she had drifted off to sleep. At first she thought the sound, abrupt and deadening, was in a dream. She stood quietly. Her mother still slept. Even Myrtle had laid her head on the side of the bed. Avanelle stepped into the other room. The men also slept. Morgan Ledbetter was gone.

"Pa," she said.

"What?"

"Pa, please wake up."

"What—what is it, honey?"

"Mr. Ledbetter is not here."

"He probably just had to step outside a moment."

"Pa, I have an awful feeling."

"You're not sick, are you?"

"No, it's not that. It's just a dreadful feeling."

"It's been a terrible night, something I hope we never have to experience again. How is your mother?"

"Asleep."

"Well, that's the best thing. Try to rest. I'm sure Mr. Ledbetter will return in a few minutes."

Avanelle returned to Emma's room and McIntosh realized his Bible still lay open in his lap. He closed it softly and studied Ledbetter's two boys, asleep on the floor.

He wondered how much longer they would stay here. He had heard folks say they were not much as farmers. Ledbetter's hand was firm as lead and they would grow weary of the weight.

He waited for the doorknob to turn. Then he began to worry. He looked at the corner. He was certain a shotgun had stood in the corner. It was gone. He laid the Bible on the small dark table near the chair and stood and went to the redness of the window. Red-singed clouds streaked the sky, burned by the early morning sun. It was good to see the sun. The land was white. He did not think he had ever seen so much snow. Tree limbs drooped under the weight. He touched the window pane. The glass was like ice. The boys needed to build a fire but he hated to wake them. Maybe he would see to it. But, then, he wondered where Ledbetter was. He should be back by now. Again he looked at the corner. Yes, he was certain a shotgun had stood there. Now there was only an empty space.

McIntosh stepped outside. The snow, untouched, lay pure, undefiled. And then he saw. The footsteps, deep in the snow, did not lead toward the outhouse. They led toward town. He hurried back inside and went to Emma's room. Avanelle and her mother looked up. He motioned for them to come out of the room.

"Caleb, what has happened?" Elizabeth asked. "You look awfully worried."

The Ledbetter boys were still asleep on the floor.

"I am worried. Morgan is gone. He's taken his shotgun."

"Maybe he's gone hunting. Goodness knows—there's not a whole lot of food in this house."

"Hunting. I think you're right and that's what I fear. I'd better go after him."

"You'll do no such thing. I don't want you chasing down that man. There's no telling what he would do. Go into town and find the sheriff."

He thought for a moment and nodded his head.

"Avanelle, stay here with your mother."

Avanelle stood close to her mother for warmth. The door closed and Stephen opened his eyes and shivered. He looked up and saw the two women and smiled sheepishly.

"I guess it's a little cold in here," he said.

"Yes, I guess it is," Elizabeth said.

She went back into the bedroom. Stephen struggled to his feet, cold and stiff.

"I'll build a fire."

He put on a topcoat that was ripped across the left shoulder and went outside to the wood pile. Avanelle turned slowly and returned to the stillness of the bedroom. She was concerned about the weariness on her mother's face and she prayed that the baby would sleep awhile longer. She thought about her father on his lonely trek into town. And she thought about Prescott.

THE MORNING LIGHT CAME into the study red and bright. Thaddeus stared at the ledger and lay the pencil on the desk. He could not concentrate. His bid to the navy was too high. He was convinced of that. He had to trim it but he could not think. He closed the ledger and ran his hands over his face.

There were too many Ledbetters in the world. The world would be better off. . . .

He shook his head and faced the redness in the window. He had seen storms like this before. The sun could be deceitful. There might be more snow in Tennessee or

Alabama. If so, it would come east. He thought about driving to the depot. There would be news on the telegraph. The room was cold and he buttoned his dark jacket.

Prescott has to stay, he said to himself. He was getting too old for all this. Prescott was the only one. . . .

There was a knock. Then came a voice, desperate. And the door opened.

"Thaddeus, you need to come."

His mother stood in the doorway, her eyes tired and fearful. He stood, cold and stiff, and followed her down the hall. Galen lay on the couch in the parlor not far from the Christmas tree in the corner. Blankets were pulled up to his chin. His eyes were open but he did not move. He did not speak. And Thaddeus thought he was dead. Verlon walked up to him.

"He's breathing," Verlon said. "But he won't respond to anything. You can speak to him but he won't answer."

Thaddeus knelt beside the sofa and looked into the eyes. They were empty, a wasteland of despair, and Thaddeus bowed his head.

"Oh, God," he whispered.

"Thaddeus, what did you say?" Grandma Freeman asked.

"I'd better get the doctor," Verlon said.

"No, I'll get him," Thaddeus said. "You stay here. You're needed here."

"Take my mules."

"No. I'll drive."

"Can the motorcar get through the snow?"

"Yes."

Thaddeus reached out and touched Galen's forehead. There was no fever, only a coolness. He wanted to say something else. He wanted to say he would make everything all right.

He stood and swayed and headed for the door to get his topcoat.

"Thaddeus, get one of the boys to go," Grandma Freeman said. "Prescott will go."

"No, I'll go."

The motor roared and Prescott left the dining room and walked onto the back porch. Rap and the other dogs ran and barked in the snow. The Pierce pulled out of the barn and plowed through the snow and rolled slowly down the hill. Prescott returned to the dining room and listened. There was a stillness, a stillness he had heard before.

He walked down the hall to the parlor. Grandma Freeman ran her fingers through Galen's hair. Prescott drew closer. His brother stared at the ceiling and did not move. Verlon stood beside Prescott and put a hand on his shoulder.

"Your pa has gone to fetch the doc," Verlon said. "I offered to go, but he insisted. Are the others still up?"

"They went to bed a couple of hours ago. I don't know if they've slept. That panther put a scare in everyone. Grandma, is there anything I can do?"

"I'm afraid not, honey."

Prescott left the parlor and went onto the lower veranda. The snow spread out before him, marred by the two parallel tracks going down the hill. He looked at the sky. Already the wind was driving red clouds from the northwest. And there was the stillness, the implacable stillness. He went back into the house.

LEDBETTER FOUND TRUDGING THROUGH the snow difficult, but it was something he had to do. It was something that should have been done a long time ago, he kept saying to himself. He had walked the countryside all his life, yet now it looked different. He wondered about direction. The farmhouses set far back from the road, their roofs bearing the burden of snow, did not look the same. The fields did not look like the fields where cotton and corn had grown during the summer.

He stopped and studied the sky. Already slivers of red and gray cloud clusters flew across the sun. The brightness nearly blinded him. There would be more snow, he decided, and that was all right. The snow and the wind and the cold did not matter. All that mattered was the double-barrel shotgun that rested in the crook of his arm.

Occasionally a farmer or a farmer's wife stepped onto a porch and stared. One even called out his name, but he ignored the greeting. The tree limbs sagged and bowed before him, but he did not notice. He trudged up and down the hills, uncertain.

"I can't believe my eyes are fooling me," he said. "At a time like this."

He stopped and listened. At first he thought he heard nothing. A dog barked and was quiet. But he knew he heard something, something besides the wind whistling past the oaks and hickories.

THADDEUS GUIDED THE PIERCE carefully through the snow. The black leather seats were cold and the wool topcoat was little comfort. The dark brown leather gloves fit his hands tightly and he gripped the wood of the steering wheel. He hoped Doc Evans would be home. Maybe he was at the Ledbetter place. Thaddeus grimaced. Ledbetters. It was their fault, nobody else's. Galen should have never gotten involved with Emma, but he was sure she had led him on. She was looking for a ticket to board a money train. Galen was the ticket. But the money train did not stop.

Galen should have known better. And then Thaddeus remembered his son's eyes. They were empty. There was nothing behind them. It was as if he were dead, still breathing, but dead. No, he said to himself, he should not think like that. Galen was not dead. Something was wrong, but whatever it was could be fixed. Thaddeus had money. He could find the best doctor. Doc Evans was not the best, not by a long shot. There were better doctors. Certainly in Atlanta there were better doctors. That was what he would do. Once the storm let up he would drive Galen to Atlanta. And if he did not find the right doctor there, he would put him on a train and take him north. There would be doctors in the North who could treat this sort of thing.

He drove past the cemetery. He was glad Abigail was not here to see Galen. It would break her heart, and then she would blame him. He guessed he was to blame. No, he was not to blame. It would take Abigail awhile to see, to understand. But eventually she would—she would see that it was Morgan Ledbetter's doing. Now Thaddeus understood. Ledbetter had orchestrated the whole thing. That must have been what happened. He had put his daughter up to it. He had encouraged her to pursue Galen. Galen was susceptible, vulnerable. Somehow Ledbetter sensed it. It would have never worked with Prescott. Prescott was too smart. But Galen was not as strong as Prescott. Somehow Ledbetter knew it. So, that was the answer. That was what had happened. Ledbetter used

Emma to get some of the Freeman money. Well, he got a little, just a drop, and it was all he would ever get.

The sunshine that was so bright earlier was now fading into grayness. He leaned over the steering wheel and studied the sky. The clouds were building. More snow. He breathed deeply and looked back at the road. He saw the figure. It was a man. At first he did not recognize him. He pressed gently on the accelerator and the motor hummed. He drew closer. Ledbetter. What was he doing at the side of the road? Thaddeus saw the shotgun.

Ledbetter recognized the black motorcar. Most folks, assuming they could afford an automobile, would be content with a Ford, but not Thaddeus Freeman. No, sir, Ledbetter said, not Thaddeus Freeman. Only the finest motorcar would do, but it was not going to help him now.

Ledbetter held the shotgun in both hands, red from the cold, and pulled back both hammers. Thaddeus stopped the Pierce. Suddenly he mashed the accelerator to the floorboard. The motorcar spun forward and leaped in the snow. Ledbetter aimed and pulled the trigger. The radiator hissed like a wounded bobcat but still the motorcar came. Ledbetter looked down the barrel and struggled to hold it steady and pulled the other trigger. The windshield shattered and still the motorcar came.

JACK BARTON HAD BEEN THE SHERIFF in Kingston for twenty years and he had never seen such a snowfall. He had heard old-timers talk about the winter storms that occurred right after the war, but he figured a lot of the conversation was pure exaggeration. Now he was not so sure. Barton was in his sixties. Most of his hair was gone. The little that remained was already white. In his youth he had stood well over six feet but now he was stooped. His neighbors would suggest all the crime in Kingston was too much of a weight on his shoulders and then they would wink and walk on down the sidewalk. They would wonder why Kingston needed a sheriff in the first place, and every four years they would elect him. He was forty-seven when he won his first election. He was simply tired of farming and he was looking for a job.

He stood at the kitchen window and drank coffee. He saw no need to trudge through the snow to City Hall. He smiled. City Hall. Kingston was not exactly a city, but it had a city hall. The kitchen was cold and the warmth of the coffee was good. His wife, Carol Ann, was in Chattanooga visiting an ailing sister. He was not sure what the illness was. Probably cancer. He would be glad when Carol Ann came home. He did not like being in the house by himself. He glanced at the sink. Dirty dishes were stacked in a large blue pan. He had to do something about that. If Carol Ann came home and saw those dishes, she would not be happy.

Someone knocked at the front door and he set the coffee cup down and walked down the hall.

"Preacher, what brings you out this morning?"

Caleb McIntosh stood on the small porch and trembled.

"I'm afraid there's going to be trouble."

"Trouble? That's not something we have a whole lot of. Come on in and have some coffee and let's talk about it."

McIntosh stepped into the dark hall but went no farther.

"It's Morgan Ledbetter."

Barton's face grew serious.

"What about Ledbetter?"

"His daughter died during childbirth."

Barton ran his hand across his white mustache and he inhaled deeply.

"What about the baby?"

"He survived."

"How's Myrtle?"

"As you might expect."

"What kind of trouble do you think we might have?"

"Ledbetter left home early this morning. He took his shotgun. There's so much bad blood between him and Thaddeus Freeman I'm afraid— Well, I'm just afraid."

Barton went to the halltree and put on his coat and Stetson. He stared at the pistol and holster. He removed the pistol and tucked it inside his coat pocket.

"Probably won't need it," Barton said. "But just in case. Do you mind giving me a ride in your buggy? We can head up to the Hill."

SIMON RICHARDS WAS EIGHTY-FIVE and his family and friends insisted he could not hear well. But he knew his ears were not fooling him. He had heard shotgun blasts all his life and what he heard were definitely shotgun blasts.

"Where do you think you're going?" Lacey asked.

She turned from the stove where fatback was frying.

"Didn't you hear that?"

"Hear what?"

"Those were shotgun blasts."

"I didn't hear no shotgun blasts," she said and she wiped her small hands on her apron. "You must have been dreaming."

"I wasn't asleep. You got to be asleep to be dreaming."

"Well, maybe you dreamed you tied your boot laces. They sure ain't tied."

He looked at his scuffed boots and grunted, sat in a chair at the table and tried to tie the laces. He gave up. Lacey left the stove and bent and tied them.

"When was the last time you shaved?" she asked. "Maybe you dreamed you shaved too."

"Woman, you're a heap of trouble."

"I thought I married a man with class."

"And it's taken you sixty-five years to realize I have no class?"

"At least you admit it. I do respect a man who owns up to his shortcomings."

"And I like a woman who sees to the fatback that's burning. I'll be back."

He went carefully down the icy steps and almost fell in the snow but he kept his small, thin legs going. He saw the steam. It rose from the radiator. He struggled to walk closer and the effort caused him to cough. He removed his spectacles and wiped them on his coat sleeve.

"Well, I do believe that's Thaddeus Freeman's motorcar," he said.

He stopped some ten feet from the car. Other neighbors from the small, one-story houses along Cemetery Street tried to run through the snow. They called out to him. He did not answer. He stared at the Pierce. The back window was red.

McIntosh stopped the buggy and Barton jumped into the snow.

"You folks move away. Hey, somebody get Simon back into his house. He'll catch pneumonia out here."

He saw Ledbetter, pinned against a pine tree. The front of the car rested against his chest. Then he saw Thaddeus.

"Preacher, this is not something you want to see."

CHAPTER TWENTY

McIntosh stopped the buggy and tied the reins to the hitching post next to the front steps. Avanelle stared before her. Lights came from the downstairs windows of the Freeman house. In the late afternoon tall thick banks of clouds blocked the sun and now a still grayness lay upon the land. She stepped into the snow and they walked to the door. He knocked. There was no sound. He knocked again and waited and then opened the door.

The entry hall was dark but there was light in the parlor. Verlon sat in a wingchair beside the fireplace that glowed red.

"Verlon," McIntosh said.

The preacher and his daughter walked into the parlor and Verlon looked up. His eyes were red and he coughed.

"You'll have to excuse me not getting up," Verlon said. "This old body doesn't want to move."

"I hope nobody minds," McIntosh said. "We let ourselves in."

"Nobody minds. Stand next to the fireplace and get warm."

"Verlon, I'm so sorry," McIntosh said.

Verlon bit his lower lip.

"It was my fault."

"No, Mr. Freeman," Avanelle said. "It was not your fault."

"It was my fault. I should have gone for the doc. Morgan wouldn't have tried to kill me. If he had, I could've done something. Not Thaddeus. No, it was my fault. I should have been the one going for the doc."

"You mustn't blame yourself," McIntosh said.

"I should have stayed in the wilderness," Verlon said. "It gets lonesome, I reckon. But— Things get a little hard when you're around people. Then, again, maybe I've stayed apart too long."

"Where is Grandma Freeman?" McIntosh asked.

"She's watching over Galen in the bedroom down the hall. That poor boy just stares and doesn't say a word. I've got no idea if he knows what's happened. It's just as well if he doesn't know. Ma has an incredible strength, but it will do her good to see you, Preacher. Most of the others are in the kitchen or dining room."

McIntosh walked slowly out of the parlor and headed down the hall. Avanelle sat on the couch across from Verlon.

"Where's your ma?" Verlon asked.

"She thought she should stay with Mrs. Ledbetter. Somebody needs to be with her. There doesn't seem to be anyone else, except the boys. And they aren't much help, I'm afraid to say."

"Your ma made the right decision. Nobody holds anything against Myrtle. It was one of those things that everybody was afraid would happen one day. Today happened to be the day."

"Can I get you anything? Perhaps you'd like a cup of coffee or tea."

"You're kind to ask, but no."

She looked toward the door.

"He's not here," Verlon said.

"Prescott is not here?"

"He was the one the sheriff talked to. Pres told me and then he had to tell Ma. Pres and I had to go into town to— identify the body. Things like that have to be official, you know. Kind of a funny way of looking at it. Worst thing I've ever had to do. Standing there, wanting to say so much, and seeing—not something a person should ever have to see. We came back here. People were already coming over, bringing food. It's sitting on the table. They told me they'd sit up with Thaddeus tomorrow night. Milsaps is bringing the body tomorrow afternoon. Pres told Milsaps to do what he could, but I'm afraid there's not much that can be done. The casket will have to stay closed. A little while ago Pres put on his coat and left."

"Where did he go?"

"He didn't tell me but I know. It's the same place Pa used to go to when he had some serious thinking to do. It's that hill overlooking the river and the entire valley. That's where Pres is."

Avanelle stood.

"It's awfully cold out there," Verlon said.

"I don't want him to be alone."

"He has had some terrible losses," Verlon said. "Avanelle, you have to understand. He suffered a terrible loss today. But he suffered a terrible loss before he came home from the war. He doesn't want to talk about it, but you should know."

She stared at Verlon and listened quietly and turned. She went to the buggy and headed west. The clouds were low but the wind had died. Nothing stirred upon the snow. Behind her the house rose dimly, the lamplight from the windows pale in the grayness of the afternoon.

Prescott stood at the top of the hill beneath the snow-laden oaks and hickories. At the foot of the hill the Etowah, clear in the dying light, swirled among the boulders and dipped to the southeast. Beyond the river lay the fields that were white and would be white again in the summer, some of the best land he had ever seen to grow cotton.

The land was quiet and he listened. He heard only the voice of George Marshall in the Paris hospital where the doctors worked to restore movement to the leg.

"Patton assures me you'll stay in," Marshall said.

"I don't know."

"I know you'll do what you think is best. If you decide to stay in, report to Ft. McPherson. There'll be orders waiting for you. If you choose not to report, just wire me. When the next war comes along—and I'm sure it will—we'll know where to find you."

Marshall smiled and reached out his hand. He was a good man, someone Prescott knew he could trust. Quail whistled in the valley. He listened and found comfort in their call.

Avanelle stopped the buggy and looked toward the top of the hill. Against the gray of the clouds Prescott stood and she dismounted and struggled through the snow. He turned. Even in the twilight her red hair shone. When she neared, he took her hand.

"You should not have come," he said. "It's too cold. How did you know I was here?"

"Verlon said you'd be here."

"I guess he knows me pretty well."

"Prescott, I'm so sorry about your father."

"In so many ways he was a good man, and in so many ways I did not know him and he did not know me."

"When you were in France and I saw him on the sidewalk, he would talk about you. He was proud of you, as we all were."

"Sometimes I wonder, Avanelle, what there is to be proud of. I killed men in battle, men probably like me. And I watched as people around me died. It seems death likes to keep me company."

"You've done what you had to do. From what I've heard of your grandfather, I'd say he'd be proud of you too. Verlon told me he used to come up here to think."

Prescott nodded.

"He loved this land."

"Do you?"

He pointed to the river.

"You see the bend? That's where Sherman thought he had Joe Johnston pinned. I wish I could have seen the look on Sherman's face when he got here and Johnston was nowhere to be found."

"You know all the history."

"It's who I am. You know, Marcus came by this afternoon. He said he had to write the story about what happened. I understood. He asked if I'd like to write the obituary. I told him I wasn't sure I could."

"If you want, I will help you write it."

"The snow is so peaceful at the end of the day. You look at it and wonder that there could be any violence. I have seen so much snow, so much blood."

He bowed his head and breathed quietly. In the distance the train whistle echoed. It was the 5:05 on its way to Atlanta, and he remembered Marshall. Again the quail called and he listened and raised his head and stared at the frozen field below.

"I want to help," Avanelle said. "You look at the history of this land and say that's who you are, and you're right. But out of that history comes strength, and that too is who you are. You're strong, Prescott, and your family needs that strength now more than ever. And I will help you."

"Avanelle, I'm not sure anyone can help me."

Again he stared at the river below. The snows would melt and the river would swell and spill over its banks onto the fields and leave them ready for the whiteness of summer.

She grasped his hand firmly.

They left the hill overlooking the valley of the Etowah and he helped her into the buggy. The whistle of the 5:05 was faint. The train crossed Two-Run Creek and sped toward Cartersville. Prescott listened for only a moment. The bobwhite quail called twice. It was close. He took the wool blanket lying on the seat and wrapped it around Avanelle. Then he took the reins in his hand.

"Let's go home."

www.ingramcontent.com/pod-product-compliance
Lightning Source LLC
Chambersburg PA
CBHW051133020726
47501CB00005B/1481